Alec took pleasure in the sure movement of her fingers up and down his spine

His sides. His hips.

He'd never met a woman so certain of herself and ready to claim what she wanted. When her fingers strayed below his belt line, his satisfaction increased tenfold.

That is, until she reached even lower. And lower.

What the hell?

Thrusting her away, he gripped her shoulders with both hands, his anger back with a vengeance.

"If you're trying to frisk me now, woman, let me spare you the trouble." Yanking her wrist forward, he steered her palm to rest on the only weapon he carried.

"Thanks to you, I'm damn well armed."

Blaze™

Dear Reader,

Brace yourselves! I took a dive into darker terrain for the second book in my WEST SIDE CONFIDENTIAL series, as detective Vanessa Torres (remember her from *Silk Confessions*, Harlequin Blaze #171?) takes center stage. Who knew the tough-talking detective had so many secrets up her sleeve? I hope you enjoy my most suspenseful—and possibly hottest—Harlequin Blaze release yet. I fell for Alec right along with Vanessa, even though he's hardly a charmer. What is it about those brooding alpha males that can turn a girl's head? Even Vanessa had to pay attention...once she brought him down a notch or two!

There's more to come in WEST SIDE CONFIDENTIAL, which will be an ongoing Harlequin Blaze miniseries. You can look for the next release in the series at eHarlequin.com, or visit me at www.JoanneRock.com to learn more. Until then, please keep an eye out for *Love Me Tender*, an anthology of Elvis-themed stories with offerings from Stephanie Bond, Jo Leigh and me, coming to Harlequin Signature Select in August 2005.

Happy reading,

Joanne Rock

Books by Joanne Rock

JOANNE ROCK
HIS WICKED WAYS

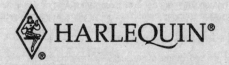

HARLEQUIN®

TORONTO • NEW YORK • LONDON
AMSTERDAM • PARIS • SYDNEY • HAMBURG
STOCKHOLM • ATHENS • TOKYO • MILAN • MADRID
PRAGUE • WARSAW • BUDAPEST • AUCKLAND

So many hands touch a writer's work before it finds its way to a reader.
I owe great thanks to the people in my life who bolster me and inspire
me to take new creative risks. This book is dedicated to Wanda Ottewell,
whose expert advice and encouragement have helped me remain focused
and enthused about the creative process over the past four years through
sixteen releases for Harlequin Blaze, Harlequin Temptation and special
projects. Wanda, thank you so much for all your thoughtful insights and
helping me make each story the best it can be!

RECYCLED PAPER · RECYCLED PAPER

ISBN 0-373-79186-0

HIS WICKED WAYS

Copyright © 2005 by Joanne Rock.

1

VANESSA TORRES didn't need to click the heels of her ruby slippers together to remember there was no place like home.

Nope, her shoes—size ten black leather Converse sneakers that had seen better days—beat the streets of the South Bronx with the same mixture of wariness and attitude that had carried her through twelve years of public school in New York's toughest borough. So what if the neighborhood had undergone some revitalization? The sun might be shining on an old men's chess game in front of a new antique shop on 172nd, and the girls skipping double Dutch looked harmless enough, but Vanessa would lay odds the geezers were packing heat beneath their game board and the preteen jump ropers had probably already been recruited by local gangs who still haunted the playgrounds.

Damn straight there was no place like home when you grew up in the Bronx.

Scavenging what peace of mind she could from the 9 mm tucked in the waistband of her jeans, Vanessa gladly endured the late spring heat through the extra layer of a linen blazer since it covered the NYPD-issued weapon. Five years of training in kendo had given her confidence in her ability to fight hand to hand, but sometimes it took a gun to even up unfair odds—a lesson she'd once learned the hard way on this very same street corner.

Shrugging off old ghosts, she studied the buildings around one of the housing projects and searched for the address an informant had given her. God knows she wouldn't be walking this block if she weren't here on business, even if this particular piece of police business was still on the q.t.

"Hey baby, you new in town?" The male shout emanated from a construction-worker type wearing an orange fluorescent vest and a hard hat. The guy lounged on the tailgate of an oversize truck while a fire hydrant leaked copious amounts of water two feet from his toolbox.

Why was it so many men possessed all the right equipment and not a clue how to use it? But then, it had been a long time since she'd had a positive disposition in regard to the male species.

Squinting at the guy's features, Vanessa placed his face. "Hell no, I'm not new here, Tony. Don't you have anything better to do than toss out tired old pickup lines?"

She stared pointedly at the leaking fire hydrant.

"Damn, Vanessa. I didn't recognize you." Lifting a paper cup from a fast-food joint, he toasted her. "Looking good, girl."

"You bet your pipe wrench." Having grown up with the world's biggest buckteeth and hand-me-down Coke-bottle glasses, she now considered her hard-won good looks as much a part of her personal armor as the Smith & Wesson. Her life now at twenty-seven was a carefully erected facade, a slick exterior to hide an inside long grown cold. "Do you know where there's a new rec center down here?"

None of the buildings around her looked like what her informant had described and she was getting anxious to get off the streets so she could head home before dark.

"Two blocks up." Tony pointed a negligent thumb before mopping his forehead with his shirt cuff. "Some city guy with a platinum card thinks he can bring urban renewal to the neighborhood with a few new basketball hoops."

"Yeah?" Could be her man. "I hope he thought to spring for some extra security."

The local precinct was taxed enough without having to babysit the new wave of cosmo-sipping bohos who moved into urban hell for the sake of low rents and a short commute. She'd taken the express train out of the Bronx five years ago and hadn't looked back since.

"You should come around more often, Vanessa," Tony shouted as she started toward the Old School Recreation Center.

"Maybe I would if the public utilities weren't so damn pitiful," she called over her shoulder, careful to protect the cool exterior she'd adopted in her career as a detective. "Didn't they teach you how to use one of those wrenches?"

Tony surely would have stood around and argued that point with her, but Vanessa wasted no time closing the distance between her and the center.

Alec Messina, her current quarry, maintained organized crime connections that went deeper than the Harlem River and he'd been missing for months. His business associates claimed he'd pilfered money out of a real-estate development project and they'd contacted the NYPD for help locating him, making Messina a wanted man.

Or—considering his background—a dead man.

Vanessa didn't much care which. She only wanted to close this case so she could haul her butt back to Manhattan and leave the Bronx—along with her old hopes and dreams—firmly in the past.

ALEC MESSINA STARED into his uncle Sergio's face and knocked the older guy clear into last year with an uppercut.

Okay, so it wasn't really Uncle Sergio but a heavy bag in the rec center gym. Alec seemed to throw his best punches when he envisioned the family wiseguy's mug tattooed across the red leather.

Alec's Thursday afternoon self-defense students seemed appropriately impressed with the swing as they whistled and cheered until some punk in the back gave a loud snort.

"C'mon, Perez." The local kid shouted to Alec using the assumed name he'd adopted during his weeks at the center. A cynical teen with an attention span almost as short as his fuse, the youth was one of many trouble-makers Alec had roped into the class. "What good does it do to throw a punch when every kid on the block is armed? Shit, even my grandma packs heat."

Alec willed away the memory of Uncle Sergio try-ing to wheedle kickbacks out of his own flesh and blood and concentrated on the task at hand. Alec might not be fielding the big business deals that gave him an adren-aline high lately since he'd been keeping a low profile, but he could damn well teach a bunch of hard-living kids how to throw a punch. Growing up in Bensonhurst had taught Alec to hold his head high. The faster you looked like a force to be reckoned with, the quicker you earned respect.

And if there was one message universally under-stood in rough neighborhoods, it was Don't Mess with Me.

"Yeah? Too bad grandma will never have time to draw her weapon if she's facing an opponent with quicker reflexes." Alec was only too happy to mix it up with the punk in the back. If he could win over the big-gest cynic in the crowd, he'd have the whole gymna-sium eating out of his hand. "How about a volunteer to help me demonstrate?"

Purposely making eye contact with the guy—a short-tempered wing nut whose friends called him Easy—

Alec willed the kid to step up to plate. He wasn't real happy when a throaty feminine voice piped up instead.

"I'm game."

Knowing there were only five women signed up for a class with nearly twenty guys, Alec couldn't imagine which one of the females made the offer. The two toughest ladies in the group were rumored to have already been recruited by the neighborhood's most deadly gang, but neither of them had the same tonal inflection as the soft-spoken voice from the back.

A pathway cleared through his students as they stood aside to give him a clear view of the speaker.

Tall, lean and dressed head to toe in black, the woman was new to the class. New to Alec's eyes. And holy hell, what a visual treat she made. Long, dark hair twined into a neat braid that trailed over her shoulder in a silky-looking rope. A total lack of makeup gave her an all-business air while emphasizing the smooth perfection of her creamy skin. Utterly straight posture and a kind of catlike grace in her bearing made Alec think some sort of comic-book superheroine had swooped into his rec center to test his skills.

"By all means." He gestured to the mat alongside him, curious what she could want with his workshop. "Thanks for offering, Ms.—"

"Torres. Vanessa Torres." She walked toward him with smooth efficiency and none of the rump-shaking strut some women employed to distract men. "My pleasure."

Something was off. She looked entirely too sure of herself to be enrolled in a self-defense course. Even his advanced students didn't have this much confidence. Oh, they talked a good game, but there was a difference between women who said they could kick ass and women who could actually follow through. Alec suspected Ms. Torres fell into the latter category.

And although the idea of her as a comic-book superheroine might appeal to latent teenage fantasies, chances were good she wasn't some Lara Croft knock-off sent here just to make him drool. That made him a hell of a lot more worried about her purpose.

"I'm sure the pleasure is mutual." He eyed her across the two feet of distance she left between them. Even close up, she looked too damn sure of herself. He tried to catch her scent and failed, which only made him want to get closer. Much closer. "Care to tell me what you're doing in this class?"

He couldn't afford to let one of Uncle Sergio's underlings discover him here in the heart of the Bronx, doling out free lessons in a rec center he'd cobbled together on a shoestring budget. Not only did it serve a purpose in the community, it gave renegade enemies of the mob a great place to hide.

"Just trying to fill some gaps in my knowledge." She smiled as she rolled up her sleeves. "That okay with you, Mr.—?"

"Perez." The name barely stuck in his throat after six months of living anonymously. Damn, but he wanted to reclaim his life. He had a thriving real-estate business to oversee. Clients with big projects and deep pockets who would pay well for his brand of expertise. And beyond that, he'd like to spend a little time indulging more personal wants.

A very particular hunger sprang to mind as he stared at Ms. Torres and her cool-as-you-please dark gaze.

A snort of laughter from Easy made Alec realize he'd probably stared too long. Damn it. Time to get back to work and hope this newcomer wasn't on his uncle's payroll. He had enough on his plate here without dealing with mob types bent on revenge.

"Why don't we make like you're going for your gun to take me out," he explained, lining himself up with Vanessa. "And we'll demonstrate how quick reflexes can even the odds."

Nodding, Vanessa swept her long braid behind her back and reached into her jacket as if pulling a weapon from inside.

Alec gripped the arm in motion, stabilizing the hand an attacker might have used to draw a weapon. Unfortunately, that left her other hand free, which she promptly used to jab him in the gut.

What the hell?

Morphing out of exhibition mode and into street mindset, Alec refused to let this woman—a hard-hitting new breed of Mafia princess?—get the drop on him. Lowering his shoulder, he used sheer brute force to lift her off her feet and plow her to the mat.

His next view of her was looking down at her flat on her back. A damn fine position for her, if he did say so himself.

Too bad he couldn't enjoy it nearly long enough. Before he could talk through the finer points of his victory to his class, Vanessa kicked his legs out from underneath him, toppling him to the mat.

"Shit." His curses ran to the far more colorful in his head, but he was pretty sure that was the only one that managed to escape his mouth. If he hadn't possessed lightning quick reflexes, Ms. Torres probably would have ended up with his shoulder planted painfully between her breasts when he fell.

Lucky for her, he got his hands out just in time to keep him from smashing into her. Bracketing her arms with his palms to the mat, Alec held his weight off her as he stared down into assessing brown eyes.

"Lesson number one, don't expect your opponent to fight fair." Vanessa huffed the words into the mixture of panting breaths between them, but Alec had no doubt the whole class heard.

He'd bet his personal jet that the demonstrations had never been this interesting before.

He held himself there, taking in the soft wash of color on Vanessa's cheeks, the lone strand of displaced dark hair twining over her neck. At last he caught her scent—a classic, simple tea rose completely unsuited for a woman who probably ate purse snatchers for lunch.

Clearing his throat, he lowered his voice. "And lesson number two, self-defense is more fun than it looks."

The comment hadn't really been intended for the rest of the class. But somehow, stretched out over top of her, it was easy to forget they had an audience.

"Oh, it's looking pretty fun," some wiseass bystander felt compelled to remark.

Low laughter rumbled through the onlookers.

Damn. This butt-kicking phenomenon—Vanessa—didn't deserve that. She'd neatly beaten his ass, fair and square, so it seemed sort of tacky to undermine the accomplishment with cheap sexual innuendo.

Propelling himself up, he shoved away from her and found his feet. Time to get his class under control and find out exactly what Vanessa Torres wanted here. Outsiders didn't just stumble on the Old School Rec Center by accident. Since she didn't need self-defense lessons, chances were good she'd come here looking for him.

That spelled trouble any way he read it.

"I think that's enough of a demonstration for tonight." He extended a hand to his visitor but she ignored it, rolling to her side before pushing to her feet. "Class dismissed."

His students shuffled out with their usual too-cool posturing, but there was a definite energy in the air as they chattered about class and compared stories of street fights they'd seen.

Far too many considering most of them were half his thirty years.

"You've got some nice moves, Messina." The woman's throaty voice called to mind barroom hookups and all-night sex.

"Yeah?" He allowed his gaze to roam over her thoroughly, taking in every last detail of her skinny black jeans and formfitting T-shirt beneath her jacket, concentrating on the way the stark fabric possessed no embellishment beyond her lean curves. "There's more where they came from, but I'll bet you get that all the time."

She lifted one arched eyebrow, her expression betraying nothing about who she was or what she wanted from him. He wasn't worried about her, per se, but he knew better than to underestimate her twice in one afternoon. Especially since he'd discovered an interesting little secret about her when they'd been romping around the mat.

"Let me rephrase that. Your moves are pretty good for a Manhattanite." She picked up a fallen leaflet about his class that one of his students must have left behind.

"Are you trying to call me uptown?" Damned if he knew why that offended him so much. Truth be told, he'd spent most of his adult life in midtown ever since he'd made his first million. "I grew up in Bensonhurst."

A fact that she would know if she were some up-and-coming Mafia chick sent by Sergio. But wasn't the mob too chauvinist to send a woman to do their dirty work? Alec didn't have a clue anymore.

"You may have been born there, but you don't fight like Brooklyn."

"And you're such an expert on hand-to-hand combat?" He'd always prided himself on shunning the chauvinistic leanings of his family, but he had to admit the only thing that soothed his frustrations right now was to picture Ms. Torres beneath him again.

Only this time, she was naked.

"I'm hardly an authority, but it doesn't take much imagination to see that you've been away from street fighting for a long time. Your technique is more textbook than passion."

Had he thought she'd annoyed him before? Apparently her capacity to piss him off had been just warming up.

"Any street fighter worthy of his brass knuckles would take the lack of passion remark as a challenge." He stepped closer, prepared to intimidate. He'd be too glad to show this woman some serious heat.

"Take it for what it's worth." Shrugging, she didn't exactly look intimidated. She had world-weariness down to an art form. "All I'm saying is that no street scrapper would have let me get in those kind of sucker-punch moves. Those types expect the dirty moves before wasting energy on the best technical defense."

"Let's not forget who came out of our little wrestling match on top." Aggravated with all the verbal dancing around, he decided to get to the heart of the matter. And this time, he'd use some passion, damn it. Snaking a hand around her wrist, he held tight. "Care to tell me why you're here and why you came to my class toting a piece?"

Stiffening in his grasp, she couldn't mask the rapid heartbeat pulsing through her veins just beneath his thumb. Her soft skin and slender arm were more delicate than he'd expected.

"Care to keep your hands to yourself?" Her voice was steady and even, so cool and controlled he would never have guessed what turmoil lurked beneath the surface if not for the proof of that fiery throbbing against his skin.

Slowly, he released her, alert to her every move. Did her pulse race because she was nervous and had something to hide? What if she'd come here to conduct a hit—a trained assassin with great tits and a heart that fired as fast as her trigger finger? He tensed, waiting.

"As long as you keep your hands where I can see them, Ms. Torres, I'm happy to keep mine to myself." Forcing his arms to relax at his side, he calculated the distance to his own gun tucked in a desk drawer inside his office a few feet away. He could take her easily without the help of his weapon, but it didn't hurt to have a backup plan. Especially since she might have her own backup nearby, ready to take him out if she failed.

"Oh, but I think I have something else you're going to want to see." Her grin showed off straight white teeth, and he couldn't remember ever thinking a woman's incisors were sexy.

And how screwed up did it make him to drool over a probable hit woman? He wondered how many other saps were getting a hard-on for this chick even in the last moments before she popped them.

"I'm sure there are a lot of guys who would love nothing better than to sign on for whatever you care to show off, lady, but I'd rather keep my head on my shoulders a few more days." His gaze dropped to her lean curves showcased in hip-hugging jeans. The jacket she wore parted like the damn Red Sea around a spectacular rack. "Why don't you just *tell* me what you want to show me?"

Her fingers flexed at her side. Clearly, she wasn't accustomed to sitting still.

"Believe me, it makes more of an impression as a visual." She paused, perhaps waiting for him to give her the green light to make a move.

She might as well be waiting for all the lights to turn green down Lexington Avenue. He had no intention of staring her down over the barrel of her gun.

Finally, she sighed. "It's in my pocket."

Smart woman. He stepped closer, fully prepared to pat down every inch of anyone who set foot in his center with a concealed weapon. The fact that the patting would be a pleasure in this case made no difference.

"Right or left?" He hovered a few inches away from her, catching occasional whiffs of her rose scent.

Her pupils dilated, darkening her brown eyes to near black. The heat between them ratcheted up a few degrees and Alec would be lying to himself to say it was just nerves.

"Right." Her throaty voice scratched into an even lower register, the word pummeling his sense of caution into stark need. Desire.

He reached into the pocket, his fingers grazing her jeans through the thin fabric of her jacket. If she hadn't been wearing clothes, the incidental touch would have landed a few delicious inches from the juncture of her thighs.

Sweat trickled down his back.

Fingers closing around a leather case, he retrieved what felt like a wallet. Counting himself fortunate to have survived the close encounter without her pulling a gun or him falling under her sensual spell, Alec stepped back and flipped open the leather billfold.

Revealing an NYPD badge.

"Shit." The realization thundered through his brain with all the subtlety of a summer riot.

"You're now a wanted man, Alec Messina." Her words showered over him with stinging clarity. "I think you'd better come with me."

2

VANESSA COULDN'T DECIDE what freaked her out more—the fear of Alec Messina pinning her the moment she reached for her weapon, or the definite twinge of magnetism that flared whenever he ventured into her personal space. As a loner cop with plenty of training on the job, Vanessa didn't have much experience with either emotion—the fear or the attraction. She'd been functioning on clear, cold logic for so long now, she didn't know how to deal with the sudden influx of heated feelings. Fear, passion, anger—they were always other people's problems.

"You're NYPD?" Alec didn't study the badge, saving his scrutinizing for a slow appraisal of her person.

She stared right back, knowing instinctively she needed to give as good as she got with this man or he'd try to roll right over her. What she saw didn't compute to a handsome man. His features were too strong and prominent, his nose too large and his eyebrows too thick. Yet somehow on him, with his oversize height and chiseled muscles, it all worked. Well.

"A detective, actually. And one of New York's finest, at that." Vanessa tipped an imaginary cap in his direction, hoping to diffuse the tension. "You're wanted for questioning in extortion charges filed by your business partners in McPherson Real Estate Development. If you'll just come with me—"

"A city cop. Un-freaking-believable." He tossed her badge back with an easy flip of the wrist. "Are you on my uncle's payroll?"

"Not unless you're the mayor's nephew." She tucked her badge back into her pocket, struggling to follow his mercurial mood. He seemed more distant now, but she supposed that made sense given his family's long-standing animosity for law enforcement. "But we can chat more about it on the way to my precinct."

She jerked a thumb toward the door, more than ready to leave 172nd Street behind. If only she could get Alec into a squad car and down to the station, she could scratch this case off her docket and consider an old debt to Lieutenant Durant paid.

The pending extortion charges against Messina were more an FBI matter, but nothing formal had been filed yet. Alec's business partners had just wanted the police to find him. Bring him home. She had no idea if their method of dealing with uncooperative associates resembled mob justice, but Vanessa knew she wouldn't want to be in Alec's shoes when he returned to Manhattan.

Then again, maybe he thought he'd just silence her now rather than risk being found by his family.

Not that he stood a chance.

"I'm wanted for police questioning." He reached for a basketball in a wire bin full of sports equipment on the perimeter of the gym. "In other words, you don't have jack to pin on me, but you think if I come down to the station for an hour you'll be able to maneuver me into a confession with some good-cop/bad-cop antics, right?" He spun the basketball on his fingertip, steadying his elbow beneath the moving weight. "Thanks, but I'll pass."

Mesmerized by the old playground trick, Vanessa figured as long as his hands were busy with the ball, he couldn't very well pull any surprise attacks. Unfortunately, the play of his deft, strong fingers didn't do anything to stifle the unfamiliar tension still coiling through her.

"Don't you want to clear your name? Let your business partners know where you've been?"

"If I wanted them to find me, I would have told them before now." His free hand whipped the ball faster and faster until it became a blur of orange. "But thanks for letting me know about the trouble over there. I'll get in touch with them soon and figure out something."

"They're pointing fingers at you." She peered around the gym to make sure they were still alone. Keeping her wits about her around this man took enough of her attention without adding any hidden lurkers to the mix. His students had all filed out onto the street earlier, but she knew there were other entrances to the building.

Had in fact scoped them out before she'd insinuated herself in the self-defense class.

"I'm cheating my own company out of money?" He stopped the ball in midspin and tucked it under his arm. "Makes me wonder why I've been busting my ass for nine years to build a good business."

"Maybe it's all just a misunderstanding." She didn't care how things settled out, she just wanted to do her part and get it over with. "If you could come down to the police station—"

"No." He invaded her space, leaning close to get the message across. "Not gonna happen. You've got a pretty badge there, lady, but for all I know you're as crooked as small-town politics."

"You're related to one of the biggest mobsters on the eastern seaboard and you're afraid *I'm* crooked?" Didn't that beat all? "If you're so concerned, why not just call the police station and have them send a car for you? We can have someone here in ten minutes at the most."

A perfectly logical plan to circumvent his concerns. Unfortunately, he didn't seem convinced.

"Look, I'm not going to the police station on principle, even if I thought you were for real and you threw in a full body massage on the ride over."

"Not in this lifetime, *Al.*" She lingered over the shortened version of his name he'd been using to hide out in plain sight for months. "And be careful you don't verbally harass me, bud, or I'll be hauling your butt back

to Manhattan whether I have your consent or not."
Where did he get off distracting her with visions of full
body massages?

Even more irritating—where did she get off actually
envisioning her hands anywhere on this man's body?
Something was massively wrong with her today. She
knew it had been a bad idea to venture into her home
terrain, considering all the wrong turns her life had
taken here.

"The lady doesn't mind trading punches, but toss a
little innuendo her way and she gets out of sorts." He
raised an eyebrow as he lined up a three-point shot from
the side of the court. "You're not the run-of-the-mill detective, Vanessa Torres."

Don't get personal.

Vanessa knew the drill, having long ago figured out
how to keep the bad guys at arm's length along with fel-
low cops. But Alec Messina wasn't necessarily either. He
had a reputation as a shrewd businessman with ties to organized crime even though he'd never been convicted of
anything. Did that make him a good guy? Or merely one
who was very skilled at getting away with misdeeds?

"You're not a run-of-the-mill real-estate developer,
either." She watched him make his shot and then found
herself moving toward the ball. Not that she was here
to play. Far from it. She just found it impossible to walk
away from a potential competition. "But that still
doesn't explain why you're hiding out in the Bronx
using a different name."

She dribbled super casually, telling herself maybe she wouldn't need to shoot if she could keep her hands busy.

"Can't bear to talk about yourself, can you?" Alec stripped the ball away and jogged to the rim for a layup. "I have to say I'm intrigued why the department sent you out here to bring me in alone. Don't you people work in pairs?"

"I've seen your moves, Messina. I think I can handle it." She kept her eye on the ball while Alec rebounded and dribbled.

Vanessa had a partner. A great partner who would be there for her in a heartbeat if she needed him. But Wesley Shaw enjoyed working alone just as much as she did. No way would she run to him just because Alec knew how to get under her skin.

"You haven't seen anything." He bounced the ball from hand to hand, the thunking cadence reverberating in her ears as he seemed to size her up. "I had to take it easy on you since I thought you were a local with no experience."

That stung for reasons he couldn't possibly comprehend since she'd been a local with no experience once. And that lack of preparation—the complete absence of basic self-awareness—had nearly cost her sister her life.

"I'm definitely experienced." She tugged her thoughts from the quicksand of her past, refusing to get sucked into the same self-recriminations she'd been wading through for years. "And I've been around long enough to know I'm making no inroads with you unless I get a warrant, right? I'll just let myself out."

Turning on her heel, she headed for the door. No sense wasting time here with a man who just wanted to yank her chain. Six other cases waited on her desk, all of which would keep her comfortably in her Manhattan jurisdiction. She'd only hunted down Messina since her superior had investments with McPherson Real Estate and didn't want to see the whole company go belly-up. Vanessa had a knack for old-fashioned sleuthing, the kind of tedious paper trail following most detectives hated. She'd done her part by finding Alec in the first place, hadn't she?

Not.

It definitely would suck to admit defeat, especially to the man who saved her bacon by reassigning her when her first partner on the force had gotten too friendly.

Reaching for the double doors that emptied onto the street, Vanessa paused when Alec shouted to her.

"How'd you find me?" His words echoed slightly against the high ceiling.

Should she stay and hope that she could wrest answers from him without dragging him back to the precinct? To question him here posed more of a risk and kept her tied to the old neighborhood that much longer.

Then again, if she left, she'd have to tell Lieutenant

Durant she'd failed. An alternative that held little appeal for a woman who prided herself on success.

"Tell you what, Al." Pivoting silently on the heel of her sneaker, she faced him across the polished wooden floor. "I'll answer one of your questions if you answer one of mine."

IN BLATANT DEFIANCE of the heat surging through him at just the sight of Vanessa Torres silhouetted in the light from the high windows, Alec assured himself he could never be interested in a cop.

His complicated friendship with his uncle's mistress had reminded him of all the reasons sex needed to stay far, far away from all relationships outside of a committed one. Something Alec couldn't afford with his personal life consigned to a low level of Dante's Purgatory. The added knowledge that Vanessa possessed the power to haul him off to jail made his sex thoughts about her all the more unwelcome.

And blasted uncomfortable.

"You're not cutting me any slack here, are you?" He didn't want to answer her questions, but he really needed to know how she'd tracked him down. If she could do it, maybe his uncle had already found him, too.

The thought had urged him to call her back just now, when she'd been ready to walk away. If she was legit— an honest city detective trying to do her job—then he couldn't just let her venture back onto the street unaware of the danger of having identified him. She could have been followed here. Even worse, she could be dispatched now that she'd served her purpose. A chance he wouldn't take.

"You forget, I'm not here to pay you a social call." Her perfect posture looked so rigidly ladylike. He wouldn't have believed she could dribble a basketball with as much finesse as a WNBA star unless he'd seen it with his own eyes. "If you want answers, you'll have to give up a few of your own."

"Fair enough." He'd gladly dance his way around her questions in order to extract whatever information he could. Besides, Vanessa counted as the most intriguing company he'd entertained in a long time. Even if she hid a connection to his uncle bent on revenge, at least Alec would enjoy the view until she made her move against him. "I'll answer a question if you tell me how you found me."

Venturing closer, she walked back into the gym with that silent, subtle way she had of moving. He realized she wasn't quite as tall as he'd originally thought. Her monochromatic clothing and uncommonly straight shoulders gave the illusion of height, but she didn't top five foot six. Smooth skin and unlined features probably put her in her mid to late twenties.

"I figured your work in real estate gave you plenty of places to hide, so I obtained a list of properties with your name attached."

"That amounts to hundreds of holdings." No way could she have tracked him here on that kind of information.

"I paid special attention to land with active building permits under the assumption you'd need to keep busy, or at least keep an income flowing." She lowered herself to the front tier of pull-out bleachers on one side of the gym. "And it helped that I have contacts in this neighborhood who checked out the property next door to a deserted sports complex."

"Damn." Alec had been discreet in his efforts to renovate the building owned by one of his dead grandfather's cronies, slowly incorporating another decaying edifice into a revamped community center. But still, Vanessa had traced him here even though he'd been using cash to live on for months. "You've got friends in the South Bronx?"

"Contacts," she corrected, smoothing her palms over the knees of her dark jeans. "And it's my turn to ask a question now."

"By all means." He dropped down to the bench a few feet away from her, settling the basketball between them for good measure. He didn't have any intention of following a dangerous attraction without knowing more about the woman, even if his eyes were glued to her hand resting on the denim-encased thigh. "Fire away."

"Why do you think your partners have pointed the finger at you now that there is money missing from the company you own together?"

Maybe Uncle Sergio put them up to it. He hadn't seriously considered that angle until Vanessa showed up—possibly leading anyone looking for him right to his door.

"I guess because I disappeared around the same time." He twirled the ball on the metal bench, hoping to keep her involvement more marginal. "And I happen to have a blood relationship with a gangster."

"But you've always been related. Why would your partners suddenly decide now that it makes you a bad guy?"

"It's complicated." Major understatement.

Vanessa messed up a perfectly good spin by palming the ball. "Hey, I explained my answer. If you're going to half-ass your end of the deal—"

"I'm not." He studied her hand on the ball beside his. No fingernail polish. No rings. Just a surprising amount of strength. She was nothing like Donata Casale, who'd been sheltered and pampered her whole life. "It's tough to explain my relationship with my partners. All along, they've provided most of the money while I've provided the vision and actual labor required to move the company ahead."

"From all accounts, you've been incredibly successful." She didn't say where she came by her information, but Alec knew his company's projects were in business trade publications more often than not, although he made it a point to keep himself out of the spotlight. A low business profile suited him just fine and his partners were content to be the face of McPherson Real Estate.

Her hands retreated from the ball as she straightened.

"It's been a good gig." Until he'd found out half the reason his partners had joined forces with him was to leverage a criminal connection. "We were all getting along just fine until I had a recent falling out with a family member who's got some powerful friends."

Uncle Sergio hadn't taken kindly to his girlfriend's claim that she'd slept with his nephew. Thanks, Donata. She'd chosen a hell of a way to pay him back for offering to help her escape his uncle's control.

"They're upset you fought with your family?" Brow furrowed, Vanessa tucked her hands into her pockets.

"None of their business, right? I didn't realize until then how much they liked the tie to my well-connected clan." And damn, but that had turned his whole life inside out. All those years he'd thought he'd been putting distance between himself and the family, his partners had been discreetly using his uncle's name as a way to cinch business deals. They were all in a shitload of trouble now, and Alec didn't have a clue how to dig them out of the mess. Yet.

"So you went into hiding to regroup and—" raising an eyebrow, she glanced around the recently refurbished gym "—create an inner-city haven for delinquents to hone their fighting skills?"

That pissed him off. As a cop, she ought to know better. "Just because they live in the middle of a war zone doesn't make them responsible for the violence."

For a moment, he thought he saw a hint of regret in her dark eyes. But then the impression was gone, her gaze as remote and unyielding as when she'd swept his legs out from under him and planted him flat on his ass.

"So why did you come here?" Her tone implied only a moron would spend time teaching self-defense to kids who could easily be the street thugs of tomorrow.

Maybe some of them would use the knowledge unfairly. But if his fighting techniques saved a life…it would go a long way toward making up for a lot of mistakes he'd made.

"It's my turn to ask a question, remember?" He didn't have any intention of telling her more than necessary. And he found himself a little too eager to learn more about this woman who fought like she meant it and didn't waste words. Both rare qualities in women, in his experience.

"I'm ready when you are." She flipped her long, dark braid over one shoulder and crossed her legs.

Alec told himself he wasn't following the line of her calf with his eyes. He was just thinking she looked very…fit. Yeah. That's it.

"Fair enough. How about telling me where you learned those moves you used to fight me off earlier? Those aren't exactly standard issue for NYPD cops."

"I've been trained in kendo. It's an older fighting style I don't see offered much in New York."

"Yet you managed to hunt down your own archaic fighting master from the comfort of downtown Manhattan." Something about her didn't add up. The unusual martial art style. The fact that she'd found him in the first place. She seemed too well trained for a city detective. Too elite to sit around with a bunch of cynical cops all day debating how to set up drug dealers.

Which brought him back to his first inclination that she seemed more like a top-of-the-line hit woman. Probably a paranoid thought fostered by his situation, but he still had to consider it. Vanessa could be either a skilled cop who'd led his revenge-happy uncle right to him, or she could be the means to Sergio's ends.

"Let's just say I was well motivated to seek out the toughest training I could find." She waggled her fingers toward the ball, indicating he hand it over. "Now—completely off the topic—you need to tell me why you don't want to go to the police station with me."

"Don't you think that question is a hell of a lot more personal than me asking you about a few kung fu chops?"

"Depends why you were asking." She scooped up the ball and balanced it on her forearm, rolling it to her elbow and back to her hand in an easy rhythm. "I can't help it if you don't use your questions wisely."

"For a woman who doesn't like to talk about herself, you sure don't mind showing off." He plucked the ball off her arm and put an end to her trick. "And I already told you why I don't want to be grilled by a bunch of junior interrogators who think I'm going to be their ticket to a big bust."

"I recall that's what you told me, but this time, I'd like to know the truth." She watched him with those remote eyes of hers and Alec wondered if anything ruffled this woman. Did she ever scream during sex, or did that detached chill remain even then?

"You want to know the truth?" He couldn't tell her the whole story. Hell, he'd be here for days. And although he hadn't appreciated many of his uncle's teachings, Alec still practiced one of Sergio's most repeated doctrines—never talk about family business outside the family.

"I find it hard to believe you're afraid to speak to interrogators since you've been in a prominent position at a major corporation for years. Anyone who heads up the kind of controversial building projects you do has surely crossed swords with business reporters, or at least a few in-house detractors, before. So any suggestion of you being intimidated by a few cops asking questions rings pretty false to me."

He wondered idly why a city detective spent her free time watching business reports, but barely had time to guess at the answer when she barreled ahead, her low words spoken with quiet authority.

"Besides, I studied your financial records. I know you're making money hand over fist with your company and you have been for a long time." Something flickered in her gaze. Some warm ember of feeling that made him think she wasn't completely aloof. "So there's no logical reason for you to take money out of company escrow. I'm curious to know why you won't just go in to clear your name if you're innocent."

"I swear to you, I'm going to answer that, but could we break up the order of this questioning for just a minute and let me ask two of my feeble queries in a row?" A plan was beginning to form in his mind, a possible way to ensure her safety and get them both out of this mess. He just hoped his instincts about Vanessa proved on target. "You said it yourself, my questions suck anyway."

She was shaking her head no before he even got the words out of his mouth.

"Just hear me out first, and then you can decide."

"Fine." She stared out over the gym, not even bothering to make eye contact with him. "But I can't promise I'll answer."

"Do you know a lot about business? Finance?"

That caught her attention more thoroughly than anything he'd said so far. In fact, from the rapid way she whipped her head around to look at him, he'd bet she was ten times more interested in finance and business than his shady relationship with the law.

Bingo.

"I have an MBA." Shrugging as if it were of no import, she shoved her hand in her jacket pocket. The pocket with her badge, he remembered. "And a small personal interest in finance. Why?"

He recalled the sensation of reaching into her blazer himself, of brushing her thigh through the light fabric. That brief touch had been almost as enticing as when he'd been stretched out over her on the mat earlier. Perhaps because that second time she hadn't been fighting him off.

Willing away a surge of heat, he steered his thoughts back to his plan to get her out of here and keep an eye on her until he figured out where she fit into his uncle's revenge plot. She might not even buy it, but maybe if he could keep her distracted…

"I could use some help interpreting company records for McPherson." He dangled out the best carrot he could think of to keep her with him. And it wasn't a total lie. He had an excellent knack for making money, less of a knack for organizing it into the neat columns number crunchers seemed to prefer. "And to answer your other question, I won't go to the police station because surfacing now could put my partners in danger. Or me."

Or her.

Welcome to Paranoia 101. A pain in the ass to always look over your shoulder maybe, but that same tendency had kept him alive despite his notorious family for too long to set it aside now.

Already, her brow furrowed, his answers not agreeing with her. But he'd had enough personal revelation for one day and their time here was running out.

"I'm sure that doesn't add up for you, but it's the truth." Mostly. He didn't know how much that pledge would mean to her, but he'd already shared far more than he had planned. "I won't make any public appearances or go on record, but if you'd lend me a little of that financial expertise for a few hours, I'll answer as many of your questions as I can."

"Here?" She glanced around the echoing space, confusion and suspicion in her eyes.

"No." Speaking of which, they'd better get the hell out of there. Standing, he pitched the basketball back into the bin. "It won't be safe here for much longer. We could find somewhere else that would be neutral terrain."

She shook her head, her dark braid swinging behind her. "You've been implicated in a crime. Soon you'll be brought up on extortion charges. And you expect me to just take off with you to act as your financial adviser? You know damn well you need a lawyer, not a cop."

Shifting to her feet, Vanessa backed up a step.

No doubt about it, she thought he was a lunatic. Frankly, Alec didn't blame her. But she'd put them both in a precarious situation by finding him. He had to keep her close to protect her from his enemies or, at the very least, prevent her from turning him in and effectively signing his death warrant.

And he was prepared to use any means necessary— including the persistent chemistry that kept him distracted at every turn.

"I don't need financial help."

"Then what do you need?" Impatience strained her throaty voice.

Time to offer up the last trick in his bag of unholy bargaining tools.

"I need someone to take a look at the company accounting to help prove my innocence."

3

"THAT MAKES NO SENSE at all." Vanessa cocked her head to one side to see if studying Alec from another angle would help. Nope. He might be a total stud on the outside, but inside, he'd lost his marbles. "You're asking a city cop to look over your books when you're two steps away from being charged with stealing money from the company? Do you have a special affinity for being clapped in irons, Alec, or are you simply out of your mind?"

"Maybe I'm not guilty." He ducked into a small office off to one side of the gym and she saw the track pants he'd been wearing go flying across his desk to land in an empty chair. "Ever thought of that?"

What the hell was he doing? Changing his clothes two feet away on the other side of Sheetrock? He returned a minute later, wearing a pair of jeans. He carried a clean T-shirt in one hand and a leather satchel in the other.

"Actually, no." She eyed him warily as he dropped the bag to the ground and then reached for the hem of the shirt he had on.

Oh.

In theory, she knew she ought to look away for her own good. In practice, however, her eyes remained glued to the scene as Alec pulled his shirt over his head. Leaving him bare chested and...wow.

"Well, I never touched a nickel that wasn't mine." Tossing the old shirt aside, he tugged the clean one on. "And I intend to prove it just as soon as I can compare my personal accounting records to whatever doctored BS files someone is using to incriminate me."

Tearing her eyes away from the naked torso now imprinted on her memory, Vanessa searched for hidden agendas in his request.

"But I could use that information to build a case against you."

"Too bad you're not going to find anything incriminating in there about me because I'm innocent."

His raised voice called her to look back to his square shoulders and hard pecs. She hadn't experienced thoughts like this about a man in...well, almost never. She'd never been one of those types to get all sex crazed and foaming at the mouth over a guy, yet here she stood, remembering every inch of Alec Messina's chest, despite the fact that he might be spending ten to fifteen years behind bars.

"You don't look all that innocent from where I'm standing." As soon as she made the remark, she realized she was commenting more on his rock-hard body and powerful arms than his degree of criminal aptitude.

Thankfully, Alec didn't seem to notice, taking her words at face value.

"There's a lot you don't know about me." He ducked back inside his office, continuing to shout to her through the open door as he shuffled through papers and drawers. "But I guarantee if you find something in those files that suggests I've stolen money, I'll offer up both wrists for some of your cop bracelets. Deal?"

He reappeared in the gym with a ring of keys in hand.

"I'd have to be even more crazy than you to go off to some undisclosed location to read your books." What if he was guilty as hell and desperate to escape a possible prison sentence?

No. She'd been ready to walk away from him earlier, but he'd called her back. A desperate man would have gladly allowed a detective to leave.

"You think it's crazy to crack a big case? Snag a little interdepartmental spotlight for yourself?" Pocketing the keys, he stalked closer.

Of all the buttons he could have pressed, how did he know to lay on her need to succeed? That competitive streak had been her downfall more than once in her life.

But she was stronger than that now. She just had to remind herself she hadn't gone into police work for the glory. Hell no. She was here to save people like the sister she'd failed.

The reminder put a lid on her strange attraction to Alec in a hurry.

"I can't. This is more an FBI matter, anyhow." Although, the promise of access to McPherson's accounting files swayed her a bit. Not only did she fight off the need to solve a case, she also battled the hunger to bury herself in the comfort of numbers and financial data, two well-loved commodities she rarely indulged in her mission to make New York a safer place.

"Are you sure, Vanessa?" He took a step closer, his cross-trainers squeaking on the floor. "Because I can promise there will be arrests to be made by the time you figure out what's going on. And I'm taking off now, whether you come with me or not. So if you want to keep an eye on me…"

Shrugging, he didn't bother to spell it out. She knew he'd disappear into thin air again if she didn't stick with him. And what were the chances she'd find him a second time after a stroke of good luck had helped her track him down the first?

Not to mention, she'd have to tell her lieutenant she'd found Alec Messina but had only succeeded in tipping him off…

Screw it. She didn't have a real choice here anyhow. Her sister always called her the family pit bull because Vanessa couldn't let something go once she'd had a taste of trouble. Letting Alec walk away now wasn't even an option.

"Okay, Messina. You want me to take a look at your books? Fine." Truth be told, she couldn't wait. "But I can promise you, I'm not going to be sucked in by a bunch of bogus entries if you've tried to revise the data. The police department can obtain company records from your partners for comparison."

"Fair enough." Retrieving his bag, he looked her in the eye. "I've got outside documentation to support most of my transactions anyhow. I'm not asking for special treatment."

"Except for your own personal detective to solve your criminal problems." She didn't intend to cut him any slack just because she'd agreed to look at the accounts. And she sure as hell wouldn't just wander off with a potentially dangerous man without some consideration to her own safety. Gena's battle for her life had taught her better. "But before we go anywhere, I think a few basic precautions are in order."

Like no more simmering looks. And definitely no more touching. She didn't like the idea of him knowing how much he fired her up.

But she didn't plan on sharing those particular safety measures with him.

"You want to take separate cars and meet up somewhere?" His agreeable tone suggested he'd already thought of this.

And while Vanessa appreciated his idea of caution, that's not what she had in mind. For that matter, maybe she'd be better off not letting Alec Messina out of her sight. A man this eager to stay hidden wouldn't resurface again for a long time.

"Actually, I was thinking more along the lines of

making sure you didn't stash any weapons on your person when you disappeared into your office." She hadn't been able to keep her eye on him the whole time, and that worried her.

He stared at her for a long moment before the barest trace of a smile kicked up one side of his mouth. A full, sensual mouth with as much character as every other inch of his face.

Had she really thought she could keep a lock on the simmering looks they exchanged? A little more proof she was clueless when it came to men. And sex.

"Are you saying you'd like to frisk me?" His low words carried a hint of suggestiveness, as if he were proposing a romp in the sheets instead of a preventive measure.

"Don't get too excited. I'm a professional at this." At least she always had been in the past. The thought of frisking Alec and that way-too-masculine body of his suddenly made her hands itchy for a thorough feel. Not exactly the thoughts of a detached expert.

Amazing, considering she hadn't itched to touch a man for four long years.

"I'm sure you have a very skilled touch." He bent to set his bag on the ground at his feet, oblique muscles tensing against the fabric of his T-shirt as he moved. "By all means, Vanessa. Feel away."

His open invitation caught her off guard, rattling her when it should have relieved her. But the procedure that had seemed so clinical a few moments ago now took on whole new shades of meaning.

Clearing her throat, she sought for some of the distance that had come so naturally to her for the past five years.

"I prefer to think of it as a search rather than a feel." Her words sounded just a little bit breathless to her own ears, a stranger's voice in her head.

His dark eyes, an even deeper brown than her own, fixed on her with searing intensity. "Call it whatever you like, but we need to get it over with before anyone else gets wind of me being here."

The step he took toward her touched a match to the last shreds of her cool reserve. Heat swamped her, confused her, blurred her pit-bull instincts. She didn't stand a chance in hell of touching him with dispassionate hands, but how could she back down now after proposing the idea herself?

To do so would show him a weakness she could barely admit to herself, let alone a stranger. And damn it, she wouldn't bury her head in the sand and pretend that just because she felt some sort of bizarre attraction to Alec didn't mean that he wouldn't hurt her. She was a good cop because she knew better.

Swallowing the lump of uncertainty in her throat, she snapped at him. "Well turn around, for crying out loud." She made a spinning gesture with her finger. "I can't very well frisk you when you're glaring at me like that."

Sighing, he pivoted on the heel of his shoe, facing away from her. "Happy now?"

TENSING, ALEC JUST HOPED she didn't find out exactly how happy *he* was feeling at the prospect of her hands all over him. Bad enough he had to entrust some small part of his problems to a cop who could easily betray him the moment she clocked into her next shift. Now he had to sport a major hard-on for her, too?

Add it to the list of frustrations of the day, beginning with her getting the drop on him in front of his whole self-defense class.

He was still fuming—both with anger and with raw sex drive—when he remembered she stood behind him fully armed.

"Wait." Whirling on her, he half expected to see her standing there with her gun cocked at brain level, ready to dish out his uncle's retribution.

Instead, he caught her completely by surprise. A scant arm's length away, she had moved closer, her unarmed hands frozen in midair as she reached for him. A whoosh of relief nearly knocked him off his feet, and even as he thanked God for not taking advantage of his momentary mental lapse, he suddenly comprehended the expression on Vanessa's face.

Blatant sexual awareness. And even more startling—vulnerability.

"What?" Recovering herself, she fisted her fingers at her side. "You move on me that fast again, Messina, and you'll be staring down the wrong end of a barrel."

He could hardly get his brain around the fact that Vanessa had been unsure of herself for even a moment. Is that why she'd hesitated when it came time to frisk him? The heat between them?

"Actually, that's what precipitated the hasty move. When you didn't touch me right away, I wondered if you were going for a weapon."

She let out a pent-up breath, the minty exhalation reminding him how close they were standing. "You've been hanging around the wrong people for too long if you think I'd pull a gun on a man who'd willingly put his back to me."

Indignation laced her words. But she didn't step away.

"I still wondered if you might be working for my uncle." He knew she couldn't be. Not now. Not after that moment of naked emotion he'd seen scrawled across her face. "He's got plenty of cops on the take."

Their panting breaths mingled, the mixture of suspicions and fears they'd been dancing around all evening coming to a head.

"Not this one." She met his gaze with boldness, the truth of her words—even her own pride in them—perfectly evident.

"I was going to ask you to put the gun aside while you frisked me." He nudged his way deeper into her personal space, closing the distance between them to just a few inches.

"Still don't trust me?" Her throaty purr wrapped around him like sex in stereo, an auditory act of foreplay.

"Actually, I do. But now that I'm toying with the idea of touching you, I think maybe you'd feel more at ease if I didn't have access to your firearm, either." When he put his hands on her again, he didn't want her to worry he was making a play for the piece. And how warped was that for a concern of intimacy? What happened to the old days when a first kiss meant you might knock braces? Now you needed to be sure all parties put their ammo aside.

"That's okay." Nose to nose, she gave him a smile of mocking indulgence. "We already know I can kick your ass if I need to, sport. With or without the gun."

That took the damn cake.

He reached a hand up to her neck and curled his fingers under the collar of her jacket. "If you think you can wound my ego while you're breathing so heavy I can hear it, you're sadly mistaken."

"And if you think you can wound any other part of me by getting into my pants, you're going to walk away very disappointed." She parted her lips just enough to flash him a hint of bared teeth. "I'm unbreakable as far as you're concerned."

He wondered if she'd ever lost control in bed and sank those perfect white teeth of hers into some unsuspecting man's shoulder.

"I'll consider myself warned." Not that it would stop him from touching her more. Not now. "For the record, I don't give a damn if you're unbreakable. I just want to see you unravel."

Her skin burned against his palm, her lips glistening with damp heat. He would get her out of here, away from his compromised hideout, just as soon as he claimed one small taste of her.

Diving down those last few inches, he sealed his mouth to hers. Locked her torso against his with both arms until the scent of soft roses and sexy-as-hell woman drifted up from her skin. The mint flavor of her lips did little to cool the simmering of blood through his veins.

A sudden need to feel every inch of her pressed close consumed him, sending his hands on a roving quest up and down her body to draw her nearer. He nudged her shoulder blade with his palm and felt her breasts flatten against his ribs. He dipped down into the notch of her waist and found her abs tightening along his groin. Her body responded easily, her limbs toned and taut beneath the linen jacket he flicked off her shoulders.

Her muffled cry echoed through the rafters and reverberated in his ears. She arched fully against him, extending up on her toes to align their bodies more evenly. Skimming herself up his rigid erection with mouthwatering effect.

He moved his hands lower, savoring the feel of her, but she dodged his touch before he could reach her lower spine. He'd ask her about that in a minute—knew damn well she was hiding something. Right now he settled for cupping her sweetly rounded ass with both hands, drawing her up even higher as he plunged his tongue deeper in her mouth. Taking more than just a taste, he plundered all he could, just like the thief she thought him. In this much, at least, she could be right. He'd steal every sighing breath, every moaning cry and every shiver of excitement she couldn't hide from him now that he had her wrapped in his arms.

Tilting her head to one side, she gave him deeper access, more room to savor the slick wintergreen warmth of her mouth. His lips slid over hers with slow, fascinated strokes until he found a rhythm that made her go utterly slack against him.

Yes.

He took far more pleasure with the upper hand here than he would have on the gym mats earlier. Vanessa Torres might have slammed him to his knees with a kick, but he'd have her melting to hers with a kiss in no time at all. And damn, but that victory tasted sweet.

He speared his fingers into the loosened hair that escaped her braid, testing the silky length of the rebellious strands. Anchoring her to him by cupping the back of her head, Alec took pleasure in the sure movement of her fingers up and down his spine. His sides. His hips.

He'd never met a woman so certain of herself and ready to claim what she wanted. When her fingers strayed below the belt line, his satisfaction increased tenfold.

That is, until she reached even lower. And lower.

What the hell?

Thrusting her away, he gripped her shoulders with both hands, his anger back with a vengeance.

"If you're trying to frisk me now, woman, let me spare you the trouble." Yanking her wrist forward, he steered her palm to rest on the only weapon he carried. "Thanks to you, I'm damn well armed."

4

OVER FOUR YEARS had passed since the last time Vanessa had cradled a man's erection in her palm. Four long years without sex of any kind.

And yet, she could hardly appreciate the solid strength of him straining beneath her palm. Not when his dark eyes captured her attention so thoroughly.

Anger lurked there. Deep, dark and dangerous, the shades of cold fury in his brown eyes compelled her stare. Her curiosity. What gave a man such a fierce aspect, especially when he had been kissing her with enough heat to melt a normal woman's insides just a few moments ago?

Clearing her throat, Vanessa shifted her grip on the front of his jeans—and realized his hand no longer imprisoned hers there. How long had she been touching him of her own free will?

Yanking her hand back, she commanded her breathing back to normal. Slow and steady.

"That's quite a piece you're carrying." Cool and easy. She couldn't let him rile her any more than he already had.

"Yeah? You just let me know if you'd like a closer look and I'll be sure to accommodate you." Bending, he scooped up his bag and reached for her hand. "Right now, we need to get the hell out of here before somebody finds us."

Or before Vanessa jumped this guy's bones—regardless of where he stood in terms of the law.

"Do you have a car nearby?" She moved to follow him, Converse squeaking on the gymnasium floor. Night had fallen while they'd talked, and already she felt squeamish about heading out onto the streets in this part of town.

"Private underground parking." He led her through a darkened front lobby and down a back corridor full of paint cans and spattered scaffolding. "One of the perks of revamping the place myself."

Arriving at an elevator bay, he opened the doors and inserted a pass card in the panel to access a basement level. Vanessa held her breath as the electronic doors swished shut behind them, sealing them in the private, close quarters. She didn't need to catch the male scent of him, her senses already too attuned to his movements, his body.

"You think the rec center is going to make a difference around here?" Determined not to think about the fact she'd just recently had her hand on this guy's crotch, she concentrated on how they were going to get out of the Bronx.

She'd seen so many fights on these streets from the

safety of her bedroom window growing up. Her grand-mother had raised both Vanessa and her sister since their teenage mom had been more interested in getting high than taking care of her kids. Which was just fine with Vanessa since Nana was the coolest lady in their housing complex, with a good job at the local dry clean-ers and a knack with tools that made all the tenants vie for Nana's help with repairs the superintendent ignored.

But even Nana, a major kick-ass grandma, had taken every precaution never to send her girls out of the house alone. The South Bronx—especially in those days be-fore urban renewal—was a damn scary place to live.

"Why would I waste my time building this place if I didn't think it was going to help?" Alec shrugged, palms up. "You think I'm an idiot? I know what it's like here. But if the center gives five kids a safe place to hang out and grow up, I think that's making a pretty damn big difference."

She hadn't expected that kind of clear-eyed thinking from someone who must have dumped a small fortune into a facility that would be covered with graffiti and crawling with homeless people in less than six months.

The elevator chimed as it reached the basement, the doors sliding open to the dank, stale air of an under-ground garage. A small fluorescent light blinked on a cement pillar between the only two cars in the small area. Two other spaces remained vacant.

"A Mercedes and a Ford Focus." Vanessa eyed the two vehicles, the S600 sedan shouting *money* and the

Ford quietly announcing *practicality*. "My guess is an uptown guy like yourself needs the Mercedes."

"They're both mine." He pressed a button on his key ring and unlocked the doors on the big sedan. "You want me to give you a lift somewhere? If you drove up here, you don't want to stay parked on the streets overnight."

Her heart drummed in her chest at his choice of wording. They might be working into the night, but she definitely didn't need to categorize her time with him as an "overnight." No sense giving her long-slumbering libido any false hope since she planned to squash it with all due haste.

"I took the subway." She hadn't wanted to drive out here today since the locals had a knack for picking out police automobiles, even the unmarked vehicles. She'd planned on calling a patrol car to pick up Alec if she'd been able to talk him into coming in for questioning.

It might not be wise to go anywhere with him, but seeing him with those kids tonight—trying to make a difference in their lives—had squeezed something unexpected inside her. She and her sister would have given anything to have had someone besides Nana root for them, teach them how to protect themselves, just spend time with them.

"So you're okay with getting in the car with me?" He opened the passenger-side door for her, clearly shocked she would venture into his private terrain.

Damn it, she hadn't broken with police procedure

once in five years. She could afford to take a chance tonight as long as she was armed. Ready.

"Let me put it this way—you're driving. I have a gun." She edged past him, eager to retrieve some of her usual calm. "I think I'll manage."

Her body registered the heat of Alec's as she brushed past him, the spike in her temperature becoming more predictable the longer she spent time around him. She couldn't even think about the kiss they'd shared without her brain short-circuiting. At this point, she was more concerned with maintaining reasonable, professional distance from him than protecting herself from possible violence at his hands.

After all, she knew exactly what kind of heat he was packing, and it wouldn't kill her. It might drive her insane with pleasure, but clearly, she'd survive.

Then again, it might leave her as cold inside as she'd been for the past five years since her sister's body hit the pavement in a drive-by, and that scared her almost as much as the thought of finding pleasure in Alec's bed.

She didn't realize Alec had knelt down beside the passenger seat, his tall body doubled up so he could look at her on eye level, until he leaned almost into her line of vision.

"You sure you're okay?" He'd gotten close to her again. Breast-tingling close. Mouthwatering close.

And oh God, she'd messed up big time by coming to the Bronx without her partner, a rational voice of reason, at her side. She was getting sucked into old fears, old guilt and major sexual hang-ups she'd never been able to face. This wiseguy on the lam with an overdose of testosterone seemed to be shaking it all to the surface for her.

"I'm fine." She glared at him with the bitch-look she saved for criminals she needed to intimidate. "Can we get out of here now, please?"

The open expression in his eyes shuttered as he retreated, assuring her he hadn't missed her point. For a moment, she regretted her attitude, regretted the need to lash out at anyone who got too close. Still, keeping men at arm's length seemed a hell of a lot kinder in the long run than letting a guy think he was making progress with her, only to find out she couldn't work up any enthusiasm in bed.

Alec slid into the car and started the engine without a word while Vanessa readjusted her gun at her waist. As he pulled the car out of his subterranean lair and into the night, she realized the windows were tinted so black no one could see inside the vehicle. Illegally black, in fact, but she'd be willing to bet there were plenty of other cars roaming these streets with the same kind of windows. Eyewitnesses said the car carrying whoever shot Gena had blackened windows. The shooter had never been found.

The morose turn of her thoughts called her to remember Gena had lived. After a week of fighting for her life, she had turned a corner. Of course, it had taken months of grueling physical therapy to retrain her legs how to walk, her thigh and hip sustaining grave damage. She'd never walk without a limp, but the rest of her had recovered faster than Vanessa, who still found ways to blame herself for what had happened and still sought out cars with tinted windows.

Just like this one.

"Have you had this car for long?" She remembered he said he grew up in Bensonhurst, but he had to be at least thirty years old. The lines around his eyes had seen some living.

Had they seen an innocent twenty-year-old crumble to the curb?

"I just picked it up two years ago." Slowing for a stop sign, Alec leaned forward in his seat to peer down a one-way street. "It took me that long to decide it was okay to reward myself now and then."

As the streets grew darker in a less populated part of town, she realized they were heading toward the Cross Bronx Expressway, navigating the small side streets beneath the highway.

Always a good place for crime.

"And you haven't had any problems rolling through the South Bronx in a sedan worth a hundred Gs?" Back in the days she lived here, kids in junior high would pry hubcaps off cars like this to wear as medallions off the cheap gold chains they bought from a guy on the street. She'd never been sure if the look was supposed to convey status—as in "look at what expensive cars I can rip off"—or if the trend merely served to show off unusually strong neck muscles.

Vanessa had missed out on a lot of nuances in her preteens since she'd still been wearing the hand-me-down eyeglasses given to Nana by a social worker who'd wanted a smoke alarm installed. She'd spent two years of tripping over her own feet before they could afford to put new lenses in those frames. Damn, but she wanted to get out of this part of the city before she lost her mind to the past. Thankfully, the entrance to the highway should be just up ahead. Tension knotted in her gut.

"I think the general assumption is that only a drug dealer would have the balls to drive through here in this kind of Mercedes. And the locals stay away from the dealers. Either way, I've never had any problems." He slowed to a stop at the entrance ramp where a fire hydrant sprayed water in an arc over the street, flooding the road. Two sawhorses had been erected around the mess, but there were no road workers in sight.

Damn.

They wouldn't be entering the freeway here. Unless she hopped out to move the sawhorses and they could plow through the water? "You think the Mercedes could make it through this? I don't care where we go, Alec, but I'd like to leave the Bronx far behind."

Too bad he was already putting the car into reverse.

"No problem." Leaning on the accelerator, he redirected the car through the darkness, the majority of the streetlights broken. Maybe someone had tossed rocks at them. Or shot them out with a gun. "We can go this way."

The tension in her gut knotted all the more.

"Freaking Tony." Muttering under her breath, Vanessa cursed the abominable lack of effort by the local road crews as she shrank down in her seat. Thanks to the flooded ramp, they'd have to backtrack.

ALEC HAD NEVER BEEN the sensitive type. He had no clue what women wanted, and no real desire to find out. He knew they smelled good and tasted better. This one in particular.

So it didn't surprise him that he had no idea what the sizzling cop in his passenger seat wanted from him. But it seemed to his limited understanding of women that Vanessa Torres was more complicated than the average female. If men were from Mars and women were from Venus, Vanessa had probably dropped by the rec center from Pluto, her ways unfathomable to his kind.

She'd been brooding in his passenger seat for almost fifteen minutes straight, barely managing civil conversation. And now when she finally spoke to him, her only request had been to get her the hell out of here.

Alec knew a shortcut, and the V12 engine could plow through these streets in record time. He'd do what she asked, and he'd cross his fingers that she would continue to ask for what she wanted, because he could never hope to understand cryptic phrases like *Freaking Tony,* without her interpreting.

He shifted into high gear and blasted down a deserted street of businesses that had been boarded up twenty years ago, anxious to get them both someplace safe. His speedometer hit fifty miles an hour when a car pulled out of nowhere and stopped in the middle of the one-way, perpendicular to the narrow lane.

"Shit." Slamming on the brakes, the vehicle skidded and screeched across the asphalt with a squeal that could have been heard all the way to Jersey. The seat belt tore into his skin, his swerve lurching him so far sideways he was forced to view the scene in front of him from a ninety-degree angle. His head hit the steering wheel at some point, and he wasn't sure if he shouted inside, or if Vanessa was screaming at the top of her lungs. Noise blared through his ears and filled his whole head. Through the dizzying spin of the vehicle, he thought he saw Vanessa crack her head against the window.

Thank God for German engineering, or he would have creamed the other car. As they turned askew in the skid, he could see the beat-up Chevy that didn't even have its headlights on.

No wonder he hadn't seen the thing.

The smell of burned rubber assailed his senses, his sedan now cranked around perpendicular to the road. The street lamps must have been shot out on this block because the usual city lights were nowhere to be found. About six blocks away, he could see a blinking yellow stoplight, reminding him it must be after midnight by now. He reached for Vanessa's hand, needing to make sure she was safe.

Before he could touch her, the passenger window smashed through from the outside.

"Get out of the car." The male voice barked into the vehicle as arms reached in from the darkness to unlock the door and yank Vanessa from the sedan. The unseen speaker shouted obscenities while another man forced the barrel of an automatic weapon into the Mercedes.

Alec tried to launch out of the other side of the car but his seat belt was still on, his head muddled from the blow on the steering wheel.

Shit.

He thought about the .22 caliber Beretta he'd stowed in his bag in the back seat. Three feet away might as well be three miles for all the good it would do him now.

"Get out of the car." The kid with the semiautomatic shotgun crouched into Alec's line of sight, butting the barrel through the door and up against his chest. The piece vibrated with the guy's nerves, adrenaline or possibly a drug high. His face was mostly covered with a Raiders bandanna, but his eyes remained visible. "No one tries to be a hero and no one gets hurt, you get me?"

Tensing, Alec forced himself to remain as still as possible to keep the situation calm since the kid sounded scared. Overexcited. Alec's ears strained to hear what was happening to Vanessa out on the street, but she didn't make a sound.

Anger pulsed through him. Had the Mercedes made them a target for anonymous thieves? Hard to believe when most people ran and hid from expensive cars in a drug-ridden neighborhood like this. Or had Uncle Sergio's goons caught up with them? If he'd had someone tailing Vanessa during her investigation to find Alec, then chances were excellent Sergio already knew their whereabouts. The carjacking could be another scare tactic—and not the first one Alec had received.

"Just tell me what you want from us." Alec didn't move an unnecessary muscle as he spoke. He'd faced down guys like this at the center before and he had a knack for talking them down. Or at least talking his way into staying alive. But he'd never had to protect anyone else before and Vanessa had hit her head in the crash.

She might be a cop, but like Easy had pointed out earlier tonight, all the fancy-ass martial-arts moves in the world wouldn't stop a bullet if she pissed off the wrong people.

For that matter, maybe Vanessa's police connection would make her an even more enticing target. *Please don't let them see her badge.*

"I want your rich ass out of the car right now." The kid hit the unlock button on the passenger door to open the whole car. Rearing back with the gun, he cracked the barrel—hard—into Alec's jaw. "Now!"

Pain radiated up the side of his face, the weapon digging out a chunk of skin but—thank God—not firing. The back of his head slammed into the driver-side window as he scrambled for the door handle.

Crazy, edgy bastards had to be high. Good criminals—okay, *smart* criminals—never took those kinds of stupid risks.

Maybe the Raiders fan's partner wasn't quite as brainless since Alec heard him reaming out his friend on the other side of the car. Alec's feet hit the pavement, head still spinning as he sought out Vanessa's position.

Crumpled. Bound. Lying sideways on the street.

Holy—

His first instinct was to run to her, but if they shot him before he reached her side, who would help her? The street remained eerily calm and quiet except for the two carjackers arguing loudly about which one of them was man enough to handle the Mercedes. If anyone lived on this block, and Alec knew damn well there were residences above the hole-in-the-wall businesses, they were all hiding out deep in their apartments, far away from the windows. Innocent people were caught in crossfire all too often here.

Slow. Slow. The whole time he inventoried the block he kept half an eye on Vanessa. Had she moved, or had that just been wishful thinking?

Alec would never forgive himself for dragging her into his messed up life if she was hurt.

The V12 motor revved into gear beside him, the engine racing as the car skidded up the street in reverse, tires squealing with the momentum of zero to sixty in 4.6 seconds.

The car had backed up nearly a block when a barrage of gunfire erupted from the vehicle. Alec hit the pavement, diving forward to cover Vanessa's body with his own even though the gangsters' rowdy yells were already retreating into the night.

Drugged-up bastards were going to kill someone.

Rolling off Vanessa, Alec's sense of relief that she was alive mingled with a fear of what might have happened to her tonight.

"Are you hit?" He smoothed his hands over her back, her waist, as the squeal of tires and sporadic gunfire receded into the night, replaced by normal traffic sounds. A loud radio blaring in the distance. "Did they hurt you?"

"I'm fine." Her ragged breath said otherwise as she raised herself up on an elbow. It was the sharp intake of someone in pain. "But they got you. Jesus, Alec. They got you."

Voice quaking with raw emotion, she sounded so upset, so tense, it took him a minute to figure out what she was saying. He only just realized her hands were bound with a ratty bungee cord, her arms pinned behind her.

"They didn't get me. One of them rammed the end of his gun into my face, but it's no big deal." Gathering his wits about him now that some of the ringing in his ears had died down, he moved to untie the frayed cord cutting into her wrists. "I'm fine and we're getting the hell out of here just as soon as I get you free."

"I couldn't get to my gun." She whispered the words as if she didn't quite believe it, her speech far away and thready as she stared at the gash on his face. In fact, she sounded like someone in shock.

But that didn't make sense, did it? She was a cop. A damned good one who'd kicked his butt in the gym tonight.

"Where's your gun?" He hadn't felt it when he searched her for injuries. "Did those bastards take your pistol?"

"It's in my waistband." She sounded a little steadier as he freed her wrists and helped her to her feet. "I hit my head when the car went into a skid and I couldn't get to it when he grabbed me."

"At least you still have it." Beat the crap out of his track record with a weapon since his remained in the sedan. The carjackers scored a five-star haul tonight.

"But I should have *used* it. Why else does the city pay me to carry a gun?" Her eyes were anguished as she swiped a smudge of dirt from her cheek. "Being here...in the Bronx...has been messing with my head all day. I'm not thinking straight."

"Well, since my brain was effectively scrambled by the nose of a twelve-gauge shotgun tonight, we'll make a hell of a pair." Actually, he'd been far more scared of having that gun held on *her,* but he didn't figure she'd appreciate his pointing that out. His head throbbed from jaw to temple, the drying blood caking into a stiff mask along one cheek.

Reaching into the pocket of his jeans for his wallet, he didn't want to let on that he was worried about her.

Right now, he just needed to make a call and since his cell phone resided in the Mercedes along with everything else, he would be forced to hunt down a pay phone. He had to get them someplace safe before Vanessa decided to haul her sweet butt back to the security of her precinct tonight instead of hanging around a potential mobster.

As if he'd blame her.

"The gunfire." Her eyes were huge in her face, the pupils dilated so wide she looked more like a child's doll than a living, breathing woman. "It didn't hit anyone?"

She peered around the deserted street as if she fully expected a body to appear.

"I think they fired into the air." Finding two quarters, Alec scouted out a pay phone and reached to bring Vanessa with him while he called a car to come pick them up.

No sooner had he wrapped his hand around hers than headlights appeared at the end of the street, a taxi sign perched on the roof.

Thank you, God.

Alec didn't know what kind of riffraff might scuttle up the street in the wake of a carjacking to pick over the victims, but in this neighborhood, he definitely didn't want to stick around long enough to find out.

Flagging down the cab, he helped Vanessa inside and slid in next to her.

"I hear trouble a few blocks away." The cab driver

with a name chock full of consonants on his ID tag gestured to the east. "Bad neighborhood at this hour. Very bad."

"You're not kidding." Alec pulled out a wad of cash and slid it through the slot in the safety glass behind the driver. "Thanks for stopping."

"You're very welcome." The cabbie's smile filled the rearview mirror. "Where to?"

Alec wouldn't give Vanessa a chance to weigh in on this one. If the thugs had been Sergio's goons, Vanessa and he needed to go into hiding—fast.

A hotel was out because he didn't want to advertise his presence with a credit card. But Al Perez—Alec's alter ego—still had a few tricks up his sleeve. Giving the driver the address, Alec settled into his seat as they took off.

"Isn't that Trump Tower?" Vanessa twitched nervously in the seat beside him, her attention flitting from Alec to the city sprawl outside her window and back again.

"Al Perez's home away from home." He just hoped Vanessa would be okay once he got her there. "Like it or not, lady, you're bunking with me until we find out who's after us."

5

"I'M NOT STAYING WITH YOU." Vanessa didn't know what would happen if she spent the night in close proximity to Alec, but it wouldn't be pretty. Her emotions had been tense to start with and then scraped raw by the bandanna-wearing gunmen who'd yanked her out of the car. She'd nearly lost it when gunshots had rung out over the deserted street tonight.

Visions of her sister falling mingled with Alec diving to the ground. Fears old and new left the metallic taste of horror on her tongue. For a few breath-robbing seconds, she'd thought he had been hit, too.

"You don't have a choice." Alec stared at her from too close in their cocoon of back-seat privacy, his features magnified as she realized somehow she'd ended up wrapped in his arms. And yet, she was so cold inside, so numb straight through, she barely even felt those strong muscles holding her.

Her breath came faster in all the signs of a panic attack—a phenomenon that had plagued her for three months after Gena's accident. And oh God, she couldn't afford to lose it now. Not with Alec right next to her.

Holding her, for crying out loud.

"You don't understand." And with the colored spots dancing in front of her vision, she wasn't sure she had the mental wherewithal to explain. "I've been a detective on the force for almost five years, and not once have I let a situation rattle me."

"These guys weren't playing around, Vanessa." He squeezed her tighter. So hard she could almost imagine he touched something inside her. "Christ, cut yourself some slack."

His words sounded far away, yet his touch—too rough, too forceful and somehow just right—grounded her in a way no rational argument could. Taking deep breaths, she allowed herself to soak up the feel of his arms banded around her, the scent of his soap chasing away the stale air of the cab until she could breathe again.

Never before had the human touch wielded such a powerful effect for her. For months after Gena's accident, Vanessa had actively searched for forgetfulness in a man's arms. Any man's arms. It had been a painful time in her life made all the worse by her attempts to revive some sense of feeling in her numb existence.

What did it mean that Alec could make her feel something now, when nothing had touched her in the past?

"I need a certain amount of professional distance to maintain objectivity here." She stared down at his arms wrapped around her, knowing she couldn't even work

up a suitable glare when all she wanted to do was bur-
row into that strong chest and not come out for a week.
Or two. "I'm not going to be able to help you if I'm
shaken up, and I'm not saying those guys scared me,
but I will admit that I've been off my game from the moment I stepped foot in the Bronx tonight for reasons I'm
not prepared to discuss."

There. She'd said it, and the world hadn't come to a
screeching halt. God knows, it hadn't been easy to
admit that weakness to him, but she was running out of
time to convince him she needed to be alone as they
headed closer to midtown Manhattan in the fast-mov-
ing traffic of—she checked her watch—almost 2:00
a.m.

"Nobody's asking you to be objective tonight, damn
it." Releasing her, Alec shifted a few inches away. Lowering his voice, he spoke much softer than the eastern
music blaring on the other side of the cab's safety glass.
"Besides, we don't know if those guys were just your
average carjackers, or if they targeted us for a reason.
Until we figure out what the hell is going on, you're of-
ficially part of my nightmare. Understand?"

Of course she didn't understand. The spots were already returning to her vision the second he stopped
holding her. And worse, a wind colder than their attack-
ers' eyes whipped through her with icy fingers.

As the cab slowed down in front of Trump Tower, Vanessa didn't have a clue what to say. The only thing she
knew for sure was that she would probably pass out in

a few minutes if Alec didn't wrap those arms of his around her again.

He thought *she'd* invaded *his* ordeal? He didn't know the half of it. And he could just stay in the dark, as far as she was concerned, because she didn't share her ghosts with anybody.

"Fine." She'd brazen this out if it killed her because she didn't have the strength to find her own way home tonight anyhow. "I'll go with you. But just until we find out who's behind this."

Tomorrow she'd call in. File some kind of report that wouldn't jeopardize Alec if he was telling the truth. Find a way to ward off the well of cold that seemed to radiate from her gut ever since those hands had squeezed into her upper arms and ripped her from the car...

Too late she realized that Alec had already paid the driver and now leaned in to lend her a hand.

"We need to move quickly through the building and don't look anyone in the eye just to be safe. No sense having anyone remember us if Sergio's people come searching for us here." He pulled a twenty from his wallet and shut the cab door behind her. Turning to the cabbie, he waved the bill under the guy's nose and pointed to the man's blue trucker's cap. "Can I buy the hat off you?"

"No problem." Pocketing the money, the cabbie handed over the hat and took off with a wave.

"Wear this." Alec scrunched the hat onto her head

and tucked her long braid under her jacket. "And keep your eyes on the floor. That way, even the security cameras won't get a good look at you."

"What about you?" She didn't like the idea of Alec taking chances, exposing himself to danger while she remained undercover. Apparently being on the same end of a gun as him had made her more sympathetic to his situation.

"I'll be fine. I know where the cameras are and how to make sure they don't get a good look at me. We'll be on the elevators in no time." Wrapping his arm around her, he nudged her toward the building.

Vanessa told herself she wasn't wilting into him because she couldn't handle this. She was simply giving him cover by hiding half of his body with her own. Right?

Her legs felt like rubber beneath her as they strode through the gilt-and-mirror lobby. A small throng of late-night partygoers were making plans, their shared laughter and raised voices ensuring that no one else paid any attention to the quiet couple seeking the elevators.

A few minutes later, Alec let her into the apartment after explaining he sublet from a lady singer who worked out in the Hamptons all summer and didn't need her city address. According to Alec, Al Perez had worked out similar deals other years and had earned a word-of-mouth reputation as a quiet and discreet subleaseholder when many upscale properties legally wouldn't allow the arrangement. That way, he never needed to produce identification since the whole deal was under the table for the proprietor.

"Very clever." Vanessa had always played by the rules as a detective, so it intrigued her how some people could skirt the letter of the law so smoothly. She had the feeling the rental arrangement wasn't the first time he'd played fast and loose with the system. But right now, his brand of rule breaking seemed pretty tame after someone had nearly shot them tonight. Suppressing another shiver, she wrapped her arms tighter around her midsection. "And I realize we need to talk more about this, but I'm a little wired after what just happened. You think maybe we could just sleep on all this and figure out what's going on in the morning?"

Her whole body was still shaking so badly he'd notice any time now. She barely registered the details of the spacious two-bedroom apartment overlooking midtown Manhattan. A few things caught her eye in passing. An extravagant crystal chandelier in the foyer gave way to blue silk curtains and crushed-velvet furnishings with a moon theme repeated in prints all over the walls. Sort of New Age or retro Stevie Nicks.

Her tired brain tried to envision Alec sprawled on the velvet sofa, and succeeded a little too well. The picture vied for mental space in her overwrought consciousness with memories of her sister collapsing on the pavement in broad daylight, the acrid scent of smoke burning Vanessa's nose.

"You're the cop." Bolting the door behind him, Alec shrugged, his big shoulders stealing her attention as he moved. "You know better than I do how to shake off the jangled nerves that go along with getting shot at."

Preoccupied by the tall, stark strength of him, Vanessa wanted to fall right into him. Instead, she peeled off the cabbie's hat and tossed it on the welcome mat behind her.

"I'm no expert." She hadn't meant to admit it, but her thoughts were so scrambled she didn't have much rein over her mouth. "At least not in a situation where I couldn't even get my hand on my gun to retaliate."

She hated that feeling of helplessness she'd experienced only twice in her life. So cold and bottomless.

Shivering, she wavered on her weak legs, wondering how long she could stand here before she catapulted back into his embrace.

"Are you sure you're okay?" Dropping his keys onto a silver tray filled with unlit candles on a narrow cabinet, Alec tipped her chin up to the low light of the Gothic-looking chandelier. "You're a little pale."

"Pale?" If that was the only thing that looked wrong with her, it constituted a bona fide miracle. On the inside she was twisted into a train wreck. "I suppose that isn't so bad after staring down the barrel of an automatic shotgun while praying we didn't die." Anger whipped through her along with icy resentment. "And I suppose it's not a bad way to end up after getting dragged across the pavement by my thumbs, especially since I should have been on the lookout driving through that neighborhood."

She wished she could feel fiery anger, the kind infused with dynamic purpose and the power to change the world. Instead she felt herself going stiff with the chilly fury that turned a person to static, ineffective ice.

Alec braced her shoulders with his hands, making her remember the way he'd touched her before. So that she felt it right through the ice.

"It's not your fault." His dark eyes bored into hers and for a crazy moment, she found herself remembering a few details of the kiss they'd shared.

"I know better than to let my guard down for a second." Especially in the Bronx. *There's no place like home.* "People die because of stupid mistakes like that, Alec."

"And you know what else? People live in spite of them." He skimmed his hand through her hair now fallen completely out of the braid she'd wound so tight earlier today.

One of many ways she was coming undone.

She wanted to speak, to tell him she knew better since she'd stopped living—*really* living with joy and passion—a long time ago. But his touch mesmerized her, sparking small pinpricks of feeling through the numbness.

For a long moment, she simply soaked in the feel of that touch, the simple assurance that she would bounce back this time. Her eyes drifted closed, the better to savor the warm, vibrant life force that seemed to radiate from him. His fingers coaxed tiny pulses of heat, like mini electric sparks, from the darkness inside her until her legs didn't feel quite so rubbery. Finally, she pried her lids open again, and found him staring at her intently with that near-black gaze of his.

Reminding her she shouldn't allow herself to accept any kind of comfort from k'm even though the allure of him grew stronger by the second. And—God help her—the night hadn't left her in much condition to battle temptation.

"But this was more than just a stupid mistake." She couldn't shake the sense of responsibility for Alec since she'd been in charge of bringing him into the station, and the very real fear that her oversight nearly cost him his life. "This was falling ass-backwards into danger."

"Nobody gets through life without falling ass-backwards a few times." Sliding an arm around her waist, he steered her toward one of the closed doors on the other side of the living room. "Not even trained detectives with lethal kick-butt knowledge, you hear me?"

"I've trained relentlessly ever since—" She stopped herself, not willing to share anything more personal than what he'd already seen with his own eyes. "For a long time."

Toeing the door open with his shoe, he led her inside a deep room that smelled vaguely of patchouli and old incense, a scent that wasn't necessarily so bad. A king-size bed covered with a black satin comforter and silver pillows dominated the space, leaving room for a narrow ebony trunk at the end of the mattress. Gently, he shoved her shoulders down until she sat on the trunk, her overloaded senses soothed by the limited color and calming fragrance. All hail to Stevie Nicks.

"I don't care how much you trained. If you'd kicked that guy in the balls and taken him out, his friend could have easily gone psycho on us both and mowed down every glass storefront on the block in the process." His thigh brushed hers as he lowered himself to sit beside her. "You know they were drugged up on something, right?"

Nodding, she remembered the way her attacker yanked her over the concrete with excessive force. Her back still burned from the abrasions. "Sometimes the drugs give them a superhero complex. They act as invincible as they feel."

"You did the right thing." He tipped her chin up as he cradled her cheek in his hand.

Her heart pounded again at his touch, reminding her Alec possessed some sort of alchemical power over her, some magnetic force of nature that inevitably drew her close. Sensation swamped her as he drew his fingers across her cheekbone, his thumb straying lower to graze the fullness of her lip.

Awareness crackled through the old numbness, penetrating a barrier she hadn't broken even in those few manic months of seeking out male companionship in the futile hope that sex would revive her. Make her whole again.

She didn't know what had happened between her and Alec, but it was too late to deny it, and she couldn't run away now without jeopardizing them both. Come what may, she would spend the night under the same roof as him and she didn't know if she could make it to dawn without seeking out that burning blaze that lit his dark eyes from within. How could she get so close to all that heat without finding out for herself if he could work the magic no other man could?

While she waited and debated, however, Alec's hands fell away from her skin.

"I should let you get some sleep." He pointed to a door on the opposite wall, his broad, masculine hands catching her eye far more than his words caught her attention. "If you want to shower, there's a bathroom through there."

She didn't want him to leave. *Couldn't* let him leave. Not now when he might be her only chance to pull herself off a ledge she'd been perched on for five years.

"What about you?" She blurted the question without thinking. But when you were on the ledge, you didn't much care about framing your words.

If she'd surprised him with the edge of desperation in her voice, he did a credible job of not showing it. "I'm too wired to sleep."

"Wait." Her emotions too raw to sift through exactly what she needed from him, Vanessa stuck with the basics of it so there could be no misunderstanding. "Stay with me."

She could tell she'd surprised him. Shocked him even. For a man who'd had plenty of experience staying in hiding, he didn't know how to cloak his emotions worth a damn.

And if he wanted to think all she wanted was sex, that settled just fine with her.

Better that he think her insatiable than ever to guess she was scared.

SCRATCHING HIS HEAD, Alec didn't think he could be reading her right. She'd just been jumped by a street thug toting an automatic weapon, so she couldn't want sex. She should be tired. Or scared. Or worried.

Definitely not horny.

"I know you had your doubts about bunking in with me, and I don't blame you since I've obviously come onto the NYPD radar this week." He knew he wasn't really addressing her unexpected request, but he'd been on the receiving end of enough sticky questions in his life to know how to dance around an issue. "But I'm going to prove to you that even a wanted man can be a gentleman."

Hell, now she looked even more panicked than before.

"Maybe I don't have any use for a gentleman after what we've just been through." Her fingers, so slender and strong, crept over his shoulders. And although her touch remained light and silky, Alec felt himself being pulled down to her. Closer.

Heat slogged through his veins, fiery and fierce, as anger at the carjackers, at his worthless uncle, mingled with hunger for Vanessa. What would it be like to stay with her, to let loose the blaze roaring inside him?

"You can't be saying what I think you're saying." Although, as she skimmed her hands down his chest to the coiled muscles of his abs, he began to change his mind about that.

"I can." Flexing her fingers, she wielded the short length of her nails to scrape lightly along the cotton of his T-shirt. She might as well be scoring his back raw considering the effect her touch had on him. "And I am."

In his mind's eye, he made plans to close his fingers around her wrist and move her hand gently away from the heated path she traced. But in reality, he gritted his teeth against the pleasure and hoped he could steel himself long enough to tell her this was a bad idea. An idea destined to wreak havoc with their tenuous connection and come back to bite them both in the ass.

Before he could say any of it, she leaned close to kiss the corner of his mouth. So gentle. So sweet. Right up until she licked an erotic trail from his mouth to his cheek, her tongue undulating up and down in a teasing motion as if to goad him into action.

Hell.

"You'd better know, I could have been a gentleman if I wanted to be." Sliding his hands around her back, he braced her shoulders so she could hear his message firsthand.

A small smile played over her lips, the cool perfection of her aloof features finally transforming to amusement. "I'm sure you could have."

Alec guessed he had about five seconds of restraint left in him. He damn well hoped Vanessa understood that. God knows he was trying to do the right thing.

Hands a little unsteady, he used the last semblance of calm to help her slide her gun from its inconspicuous holster and settle the weapon at the foot of the bed. Then, breathing easier now that they were both unarmed for the night, he sifted his hands through the silky mass of her hair.

"Beautiful." The word stuck in his throat while he let the satiny locks slide over his skin.

Pivoting a few degrees on the chest where they sat, Alec positioned himself slightly in front of her. The room remained dim except for the light of the foyer filtering through the open door. The lone window remained covered by heavy blinds.

Still, it wasn't too dark to see her creamy skin in stark relief to the wealth of shadows surrounding her. Long brown hair, black clothes and the ebony satin bedspread behind her gave her smooth skin an ethereal glow, sort of like the images of the moon in the prints covering the living room walls.

Would Vanessa prove just as cool and distant, the way she'd seemed when she'd first taken her place on the gym mat in front of him? Or did her plea for him to stay with her indicate a fire burning somewhere deep inside her?

With one final prayer of forgiveness for lustful thoughts about a traumatized woman, Alec covered her lips with his own. She remained utterly still for a handful of seconds, her spine straight and unyielding. And then her arms twined around his neck as she leaned back, pulling him down to the satin-covered bed with her.

All at once, his body stretched out over hers. She sank lightly into the rich softness of the feather bed that lay on top of the regular mattress, her curves pressed hungrily to the hard length of him. Her heart fluttered wildly against his chest, the rhythm erratic and furious. Just like when he'd touched her at the gym.

Tunneling his hands between her jacket and her close-fitting T-shirt, he molded his touch to the lean strength of her, admiring the way she took care of her body like a top-of-the-line machine. Every square inch showcased superb maintenance, lean muscle precisely exercised for maximum performance. But did she ever give this prime figure free rein? Allow herself to see how many orgasms she could have in one night?

Alec had the distinct impression this was a woman unaccustomed to using her body for fun. Pleasure.

Or hell, maybe he still harbored teenage fantasies about strong females like Detective Torres and he hadn't come close to seeing her real needs.

Shutting off his clueless brain, he simply gave himself over to the pleasure of touching her. Slipping his hand beneath the loosened hem of her shirt, he roved his fingers over the soft skin of her belly, dipping into the smooth depression of her navel. He couldn't wait to trace his tongue over that same path. Except that, when he went that route with his mouth, he'd be going down instead of coming up.

For now, his fingers rose up to the smooth satin cups of her bra, a rigid contraption complete with underwire and foam padding. Only, the breasts beneath weren't the sort that needed uplifting. If anything, Alec imagined they'd have all the more bounce and expanse once she freed them from the prison of hooks and latex.

Reaching around behind her, he pressed her closer to his chest. Tasted deeper. She was smooth on his tongue like aged wine. Nothing sweet about this woman except maybe her rose perfume. And that, he began to recognize as more traditional and clean than exactly sweet.

If he hadn't been on the run and trying to hide out, he would have loved to surround her exotic beauty with rose petals on this endlessly black bedspread. Her scrubbed skin didn't need any makeup to catch the male eye, but he'd be willing to bet she'd make a visual feast with a little decoration spread around her unadorned body.

Sliding her jacket off her shoulders with one hand, he unlatched her bra with the other. Amazing how swiftly a man could work if given incentive. Her T-shirt followed in quick succession.

And then he couldn't do anything but stare.

A lush, made-for-sex body lurked under her athletic-style bra and layers of clothing. Full, eye-popping breasts spilled into his hands, soft and warm and tipped with tight pink crests. He moved to taste them when she stopped him.

"I want you naked, too." Her words were as clipped and functional as the rest of her, only Alec was slowly realizing that a wealth of passion slept beneath the surface of this lean, mean, martial-arts pro who didn't embellish her words or her body.

"You're sure?" God, he hoped she was sure. Still, he didn't let her pull off his T-shirt yet, even though her hands wandered purposefully over the cotton. "This is going to change everything with us. If we do this, there won't be any going back to how things were before."

"That's where you're wrong." Bending her knee along the outside of his leg, she shifted her thigh against him and stroked his ache for her into painful proportions. "When all this is over, I'll still have my job to do."

"Do you really think you'll be able to arrest a man you've slept with?" He wrapped his hand around her leg, fingers dipping into the tender hollow behind her knee. He should have known a few kisses wouldn't erase that cool, aloof streak of hers.

"I don't think there's going to be much sleeping happening in this bed tonight." She arched her back, just enough to press the warmth of her sex to his groin. Not even her jeans could mask the heat of her. "But if there comes a time I have evidence you committed a crime, it won't matter how good the sex is between us, I'll still come after you."

"Ever the tender-hearted detective." Convinced she wouldn't change her mind now, he peeled his shirt over his head and prepared to fan the heat between them as high as it would go. "And I think you've got it backward, Vanessa, since you'll definitely be coming before me."

6

BLESS THE MAN and his orgasm-confidence.

Vanessa had nearly stopped shaking now that Alec's full, hot, hard weight settled over her. Between the feather bed beneath her and the fiery male above her, she definitely wasn't cold anymore. And when she closed her eyes, she still saw Alec's face outlined in the shadowy room instead of the crazed, venomous glare of her assailant.

That is, unless Alec stopped kissing her. Touching her.

She remedied that by arching up to brush her lips over his again. Dropping light kisses along his cheek, she carefully avoided the dried wound along the stark angle of his jaw.

Smoothing her hands down his torso, she savored his exposed flesh as he stripped off his T-shirt. The lines were all male, tapering down from wide shoulders to a narrow waist, the same mouthwatering cut that football players achieved with exaggerated padding. Alec's leaner muscles might be less pronounced and more fluid, but in her mind, they were just right on a man. The kind of physique that combined speed with power.

As her hands molded to the solid strength of him, he moved lower to unzip her jeans. Ribbons of sensation fanned out from her belly where his thumb grazed her skin as he parted the fabric. The tingling response inside her warmed her from within the same way his touch heated her from without.

Her memories of sex before tonight were vague and unhappy. This was vivid, and growing more intense by the moment.

Yes.

Memories of the carjacking dulled and softened, shoved firmly to the back of her mind so she might give herself over to the moment. She wriggled her hips to free herself of the jeans Alec tugged off her, the satin comforter sliding sensually beneath her skin.

He left her panties in place, and for a moment she mourned that barrier between them, especially since he shed the rest of his clothes in a blink. She barely got a good look at him since he moved too quickly. Besides, he turned away as he peeled off his jeans, digging into the nightstand drawer for what she assumed must be a condom.

A wild, wanton noise escaped her lips, effectively calling him back to her side. He dropped a small, fabric-covered box next to her on the bed, but she hardly gave it a glance in her hurry to get a peek at him.

She'd felt him before, back at the gym, when she'd thought for sure he must be fully aroused. But apparently he'd only been warming up.

"Very impressive piece." She whispered the words in his ear as he lay down beside her, rolling her up on her hip so they faced one another. "That's a lot of fire-power you're carrying."

His teeth flashed white in the shadows as he traced the curve of her breasts with his fingertip. "You've been driving me crazy ever since you strutted your fine self into the rec center. Anyone ever tell you that you're too brazen by half?"

Reaching between them, she skimmed a light touch up the length of him and swirled her finger around the dark head of his cock. "Sure. But nobody's ever sug-gested that was a bad thing."

A thrill tripped through her as she watched his eyes roll back just a little before he took a deep breath and restrained her hand.

"Not bad." He held her there for a long moment. "Definitely not bad. But when do you ever let someone else be brazen with you?"

Never.

But she didn't have the guts to tell him he'd touched more of her already than any man in her past. She'd worked so hard to develop an impenetrable facade, she couldn't just write it all off to a man. She'd always had to maintain some little piece of herself.

Maybe that had been half her problem all those years ago when she'd hoped sex would provide an escape from the guilt for her sister's shooting.

"Seems to me you're not having any trouble making

free with my person." And that was so incredibly fine with her since she didn't want to think about anything but what happened in this bed right now. Heat simmered slowly between her hips, her thighs twitching with new longing. "Why don't I put myself in your capable hands just for tonight?"

He answered by dragging her closer, pulling her body to his across the small stretch of satin between them. His hand ran from shoulder to hip before skimming around to her back. She gasped when he touched the abrasions on her spine and his searching fingers stopped abruptly.

"You should put something on that." The stern look in his eyes warned her not to argue.

"You should put something inside me instead." She didn't want to move away from him for a second and risk losing this connection. She'd tried and failed at sex too often in the past to mess this up now.

To emphasize her point, she ground her hips into his, cradling his cock against her belly. His eyes closed for a scant few seconds before they flew open again.

"Then you'll take care of those scrapes right afterward, you hear?"

Once she nodded, he reached into the box behind her, coming back with a tall, thin bottle of pink liquid. The sole word on the label said…

"Hot?" She snaked one leg between the warmth of his.

"I thought maybe it would help you warm up." Flicking open the top, he poured some out on his fingers and then smeared the thick liquid over one of her breasts, circling around the peaked nipple.

"Who needs warming up?" She'd never wanted a man this way. Couldn't wait for him to take her.

"You're still shivering." Edging his way down the bed, he painted more of the substance down her abs, pooling a drop into the dip of her belly as he pushed her to her back.

She'd shivered and hadn't even realized it? A shadow of worry clouded her thoughts for a moment until the full impact of the tingling lotion hit her.

"Oh!" Ripples of pleasant sensation skittered through her, drawing all her attention to her body and not her screwed-up mind. "It's sort of sizzle-y."

"And good?" He licked a path around her nipple, heightening the erotic burning sensation even more.

"Very good." Her breath escaped her. Her whole body felt suspended in pleasure, the trail of heat igniting from breasts to belly and slightly beyond. "So good."

Her hips rocked against his chest as he lowered his mouth to her navel and swirled his tongue inside. Heat pooled between her legs in a sharp, hungry ache.

And this heat didn't have anything to do with his magic potion.

Tongue flicking lazily over her taut, eager flesh, Alec took his time to fan the flames igniting all over her. She twisted against the satin comforter, angling her body beneath him to help his mouth land where she needed it.

By the time he reached for the bottle again, she thought she would come right out of her skin. Nerves she hadn't known she possessed quivered in anticipation of his kiss. His touch.

The bedroom became her whole universe and Alec her world. She wanted nothing more than to breathe in the damp heat of his skin, their scents mingled together along with the sticky cinnamon fragrance of the pink liquid.

She didn't need to ask what he planned to do with his wicked bottle this time. He already tucked a finger into the waistline of her panties, yanking them slowly south. She welcomed the retreat of the cotton from her skin. She wanted to give herself over to a world of black satin and dark pleasures. Alec's world.

"Unbelievable." The raw scratch of his voice called her from her seductive thoughts long enough to realize his gaze remained pinned on her exposed skin.

Her *very* exposed skin.

"It's hard to go back after you get started on Brazilian waxes." She ran her fingers through his dark hair, savoring the silky texture. "It gets itchy otherwise."

She'd never had any reason to explain as much before since no man had seen her naked once she'd started full-scale waxes in an attempt to take charge of her own body.

"Sounds painful." He pressed a gentle kiss to the top of her pubic bone, the fleeting contact not nearly enough to satisfy. "But I have to say it looks incredible."

Holding the narrow plastic bottle above her, he poured a few drops of the potion down the center of her cleft. The glide of liquid over her sensitive places ignited a sensuous tremor, right up until the sizzle started.

Body jerking in delicious torment, she practically convulsed from the sumptuous thrill snaking through her. Dimly aware of Alec laying aside the bottle and rolling on a condom from his box of tricks, she reached for him to drag him back down to the bed, desperate for the relief he could provide.

Flames licked over her skin, lingering on the delicate flesh between her legs. Her hair twined seductively around her arms and shoulders as she writhed against the satin bedspread, all trace of self-consciousness sacrificed to consuming sexual need. Even her own hands felt like a lascivious indulgence as she cupped her breasts with greedy fingers.

An animal-like growl hummed through the room, reverberating in her ears and trembling right through her skin as Alec watched. Stretching long, muscular arms up either side of her body, he finally planted himself between her legs, his breath teasing the plump flesh of her clit. Desire swelled inside her, the tingling of the hot liquid fading in comparison to the spiraling vortex of her own need.

With his elbows he pushed her thighs wider, opening her to the swipe of his long, luscious tongue. The slick stroke nearly undid her. Or so she thought until he pushed that tongue inside her, swirling deeper until a climax crashed over her with wave after wave of heady sensation. Her womb rocked and contracted, feminine muscles trembling with lush response.

She cried out in a combination of sexual frenzy and delight since she'd never even come close to an orgasm before, but holy hell, *this* was definitely *it*.

She suspected the sensations might have ripped through her all night if Alec hadn't gently steadied her hips and nudged his way inside her. And yet, amazingly, that felt even better. The thick, heavy weight of him inside her filled up all those empty places that seemed to cry out with need when she'd hit that erotic high note.

This man…this awesome, amazing man she was supposed to have dragged into the police station…understood her body a hundred times better than she ever had. Vaguely frustrated with herself since she couldn't offer him the same kind of experience in return, she settled for gripping his shoulders and holding on for the ride. Every woman deserved a chance to watch and learn, right? Or better yet, to *feel* and learn.

"So good. So good. So amazingly good." She chanted her pleasure in his ear, her whole body silently singing the same song as she clung to him.

He slid away from her slightly, only to thrust deeper, his body discovering more and more of her every time. The scent of sex and cinnamon and patchouli drifted around her, giving her a sort of sex-high each time she inhaled.

Fingers twining in his hair, she spread hungry kisses

and gentle bites along his neck and down to his shoulder. The salty taste of him could have fed her for days. She could live on this.

He stared down at her through the shadows, eyes glittering and intense before he gave her a crushing kiss that tasted like sex and candy.

"Wrap your legs around me." The harsh order rasped over her lips when he paused.

Responding automatically, she locked her ankles behind him, clamping herself to him as he lifted her up and off the bed. His muscles bunched and stretched as he walked her over to a dresser by the window and shoved aside everything sitting on the surface. Knickknacks and trinkets clattered to the carpeted floor.

The sound registered as little more than white noise to senses consumed with Alec. Thighs splayed on the polished ebony surface, she let her legs dangle against the drawers while her arms still looped about his neck. She'd barely found her balance when he nudged her closer to the edge, positioning her right where he wanted.

She watched him shift her, his long, sinewy torso stationed in the narrow shaft of light from the hallway filtering through the door. The golden wash of color gave him a fantasy quality, heightening the sensation that the night was a seductive dream.

Scoring her nails lightly over his back, she held on tight as he pushed deep inside her. Again. Pleasure rolled over her, the heat thick and fierce. The drawers rattled in their compartments, the wood banging lightly with every new thrust. Vanessa shook inside and out, body responding to the delicious, rhythmic slide of his.

Planting her palms on the wooden dresser top behind her, she pressed her hands into the grain and arched back. Drove herself down the hard ridge of his cock.

Over and over.

So good.

She didn't understand why she'd never been able to really enjoy sex before—and she definitely didn't understand why the man to show her what she'd been missing had to be connected to organized crime—but right now, none of it mattered. The pure chemistry was irrefutable.

She'd climbed her way up to that treacherous sensual peak again, the swell of warm desire building to overwhelming heights. Just when she thought she'd hurtle over the edge, Alec hooked an elbow beneath her knee and lifted her thigh. Pressed himself home even deeper.

Heat blossomed inside her like gasoline on a fire, the whoosh of blood through her veins so intense her body stilled from the force of it. For long moments she remained frozen there, hypnotized by the sweet pulse of pleasure, until at last she slumped forward, exhausted.

Somewhere in the back of her mind, she suspected that she would regret her weakness tonight since falling into bed with Alec Messina probably didn't rank as one of her smartest moves. But while she might mourn her inability to put her sister's accident behind her and free herself from the past, she couldn't truly regret sleeping with Alec. He'd ignited a flame inside her that had never burned through her before, and it wasn't just the hum of sexual pleasure. Although that was a hell of a gift, too.

His touch had reawakened her, brought her to life. Whatever had been cold and dead inside her had smoldered to fiery ashes tonight in some kind of sexual alchemy. She knew this not because her heart slammed against her chest or because sweat beaded along her hairline. No, she knew because silent, scorching tears suddenly trickled from eyes that had forgotten how to cry.

WATER SPILLED OVER ALEC in the shower the next morning, the hot pulse not coming close to cleaning away the fear he'd screwed things up. Reaching for the blue washrag he'd slung over the soap dish, he tried not to think about the way Vanessa had bolted from bed this morning, sprinting for the shower before they could talk.

He hadn't wanted to bother her with any questions last night, knowing she was tired and wary after the carjacking. After they'd made the earth move and basically rewritten everything he'd known up until then about sex, he'd carried her from the dresser back to bed in silence, only allowing himself to hold her while she fell asleep.

Now, as he rinsed off the last of the soap, he found

himself facing an awkward morning-after conversation. That would have been bad enough on its own, but he had to pile on a discussion about his real-estate company and all the awkward family politics he'd been dancing around for years.

Oh joy.

Shutting the water off, he stepped out of the shower and confronted a quiet apartment along with a scary thought. What if she wasn't even around this morning to have those conversations with him? Could she have ditched him and exposed his hideout while he showered?

Knotting a towel around his waist, he stormed from the guest bathroom into the living area, hating the ominous quiet. Where was she? Scanning the empty modern kitchen and the deserted couches in the living room, his gaze moved to the bank of windows…and the pair of bare feet just barely visible behind the floor-length drapes.

Relief swished from his lungs in a sigh before he could slip back into the bathroom to dress.

"Alec?" Vanessa drew aside the heavy curtains to peer at him across the room. Silhouetted by the late morning sun, she wore her jeans from the day before and a white tank top that showed off more of her lightly tanned skin. "Hope you don't mind I grabbed something out of the closet off the bathroom. I didn't want to bother you while you were still sleeping." Her gaze dropped down to his towel and she smiled. "But you look very much awake now."

Cursing his decision to race out here in a few square feet of terry cloth, he didn't need to look to know what captured her attention. "Guess I'm still thinking about a few pleasant dreams I had last night."

The smile disappeared from her face as quickly as it had arrived. "I didn't have any dreams, but thanks to you, I didn't have any nightmares, either." Moving away from the window, she took a few steps into the living room. "Those guys creeped me out more than I wanted to admit, and I appreciate you…helping me forget about it."

His ego and his hard-on both crashed a little at that news. He was her private diversion for the night? An entertainment she'd only stoop to using after her life had been threatened? Didn't exactly sit well after he'd convinced himself he'd blown her mind in bed last night. He thought they'd been drawn to one another because of a mutual, un-freaking-believable attraction, not some desire to hide from what had happened.

"You wouldn't have a pulse if it didn't rattle you to be dragged out of a car and held at gunpoint." If she could downplay it, so could he.

"I tried calling my partner to report what happened privately, but I got his voice mail. I think we need to check out the guys who took your car so we can find out if they acted alone or if someone else hired them." She looked him in the eye most of the time, but then her gaze slipped south again. "You know, maybe this would be easier to talk about if you weren't strutting around here in a towel?"

"Am I turning you on?" Amazing how resilient a hard-on could be with a woman staring at your johnson.

"I'm going to ignore that." Backing up a step, she pushed the power button for a flat-screen television mounted across from the couch. "You let me know when you're ready to converse like a civilized…"

Her words faded away as a newscaster's voice intruded on them in stereo surround sound.

"…if convicted on all counts, Sergio Alteri faces fifteen to twenty years in prison."

Alec lunged for the remote.

"Holy hell." He pressed buttons with a vengeance in an attempt to find out more on another station.

"Your uncle's been arrested?" Vanessa sank to the couch, eyes glued to the screen.

Alec couldn't answer. Didn't know. His uncle Sergio had been a mainstay in his life from the time he was born. The guy had taken him to his first Mets game. Introduced him to the joys of salted peanuts and screaming yourself hoarse for the home team. He'd loved and hated the guy at different times, their relationship tainted by Sergio's crimes and a lifetime's worth of pressure to take up the profession.

Within twenty minutes, they'd gleaned all they could from every New York television station and the Internet, which Alec accessed from his laptop while they watched TV. Sergio had been picked up in Brooklyn by the DEA, along with five other alleged major drug suppliers in the city. Evidence suggested an important deal had been in the works the night before.

"Don't you think this news negates the theory that those guys last night worked for your uncle?" Vanessa's blank gaze fixed on a commercial for cat food.

"How so?" He clicked through a few more keys and checked his e-mail, hoping to scrounge up more information on the man who'd overshadowed his whole life. His uncle could have gotten wind of Alec's partners contacting the police. Could have easily had Vanessa followed last night when she'd found Alec, and then sent the carjackers to scare the hell out of them.

Make him sweat his decision to turn his back on his Alteri blood.

"Why would Sergio have arranged the carjacking last night if he had a drug shipment to oversee at the same time?"

"He's one of the most successful guys in the business on the East Coast." Alec lowered the screen of his laptop and set it aside so he could get dressed. Even the news of his uncle's arrest didn't make him stop thinking about Vanessa, especially with her bare arm resting on the couch a foot away from his half-naked thigh. "I'm sure he knows how to multitask."

"If he's so successful, don't you think he knows better than to take unnecessary risks when he has a big deal on the line?" She reached for his computer. "Do you mind if I use this to submit a description of the guys who took your car to my partner?"

Hell yes, he minded.

"If you report what happened, the cops are going to know you were with me since the sedan is in my name." He wasn't sure what scared him more—the fear of someone coming after her, or the possibility of her betrayal after they'd set the whole damn apartment on fire last night.

"I'm not going to file a formal report." Her grip tightened on the laptop, determination alive and kicking today, apparently. "Just launch a few discreet inquiries so we can figure out who's after you if it's not your uncle Sergio."

"You want answers?" Frustration fired through him as he remembered she didn't trust him worth a damn. Last night hadn't changed a thing between them. "I don't need any report back from your cop friends to tell me who's after us. Now that Sergio is behind bars, the possibilities just narrowed considerably."

"Then enlighten me." Straightening on the sofa, she stared him down in the mellow morning sunlight streaming through the high-rise apartment. "Because I'm going to have a taste for retribution just as soon as we find out who's responsible."

"Retribution?" He knew she carried a badge, but she sounded more like a criminal. "Don't you mean justice?"

"I mean it, Messina. Who's behind the carjacking?" Her words practically vibrated with fire and passion. How could he have ever thought this woman would be cold?

"Remember I wanted you to come with me last night so you could review some of my real-estate company's records?" Tugging the towel securely around his waist, he stood. "Maybe it's time you took a look."

7

"WHAT ARE WE WAITING FOR?" Vanessa couldn't have grabbed hold of the idea any faster if she'd been drowning and Alec had offered her an inflatable Shamu.

And since she was drowning in her own reawakened sensuality this morning, her heightened sexual awareness flooding her with a million lust-inspired thoughts, the analogy wasn't too far off base. She should be scared for her life, holed up in this apartment with a man wanted dead by some of the scariest criminals in the city, and yet the predominant thought in her head today was how this unlikely lover had brought her back from an impossibly dark ledge.

A feat that hadn't been accomplished with the passage of five long years. A feat that really good therapy hadn't managed.

Alec stared at her with hooded eyes, the heat swelling between them already and they'd barely been out of bed for an hour. She thought he might kiss her. God help her, she wanted him to kiss her. But he turned abruptly on his heel.

"I'll be right back." He disappeared into the other

bedroom, the one she hadn't seen the night before, only to return a minute later wearing an unbuttoned white dress shirt and charcoal-gray trousers. His wet hair grazed the crisp collar of the shirt, his chest still exposed to her gaze. "The business accounting records were stolen last night along with the car, but I have some other proof that McPherson is running some shady deals."

With an effort, she yanked her eyes and thoughts away from Alec's chest to focus on the manila folder he thrust under her nose.

"Do you have copies of those accounting reports anywhere?" Her heart lurched at the thought of lost evidence, recognizing the importance of a paper trail in building a case.

"Yes." He tugged over an ottoman with his foot until it rolled right up to the back of her calves. "But not here, and for now, it's too risky to retrieve them until we have a better handle on who might be trying to find me and why."

Sinking into the dark brocade of the long footrest, Vanessa cracked open the folder to find copies of e-mails dating back nearly a year ago. Conversations between Alec and someone with a computer-screen name of…

"Kittykat?" She didn't want to contemplate the tight ache of jealousy that stabbed through her at notes that went beyond friendly to outright flirtatious. Especially on Kittykat's side, since she liked to sign off with the endearment "Your Pussy."

"She saw something between us that wasn't there." Alec lowered himself into a chair beside Vanessa and flipped through the messages to one dated just before last Christmas. "The woman is Sergio's mistress and the only reason I talked to her at first was because she feared for her life. Later, she implied she had access to information about my business partners."

Vanessa's first instinct told her to slam the folder shut and throw all discussion of this woman back in his face, but she refused to allow petty emotions to affect her job. She would find out who wanted Alec dead, even at the expense of newly raw emotions.

"She says here that McPherson and Vercelli have been in contact with Sergio about your business?" Vanessa scanned the note, trying to follow the conversation without dwelling on all the extraneous endearments and suggestions they have dinner. She hated Kittykat without ever laying eyes on the woman.

"My partners in the real-estate development company—William McPherson and Mark Vercelli." Alec planted his elbows on his knees, his open shirttails dangling between his sprawled legs. "Donata swore to me they'd approached my uncle about tying the business to Sergio's criminal contacts, something I'd refused to do from the moment we incorporated."

"Let me get this straight." Vanessa turned to Alec, surprised by how close he sat. She could kiss him. Touch him. Lure him back to bed instead of untangling the mess of complications in his world. "Your partners *want* to work with the mob? I thought no one in his right mind willingly got involved with that kind of stuff."

Then again, maybe Alec's partners had questionable ties to crime, too. Vanessa hadn't even done a rudimentary check into their backgrounds, trusting her senior officer to have completed his homework on the guys. Actually, now that she thought about it, maybe her lieutenant hadn't delved into the legitimacy of these partners since he'd mentioned having investments with the real-estate company himself.

"Depends how greedy you are." Alec stared blankly at the TV, frustration evident in his clipped words. "There's a lot of money to be made off illegally obtained contracts and prices inflated by crime. Maybe my partners were swayed by the bottom line."

"But you've worked with them for a long time, right?" Vanessa peered inside the folder again, suspicious of anything written by the uncle's mistress who obviously had the hots for Alec. Had she ever swayed him into her bed? "Do you believe they could have been persuaded to the other side?"

"I've known Vercelli since college and find it hard to believe he'd be able to pull this off. But I caught McPherson signing out some of my archived expense reports. I made copies of all the accounting records I could before I disappeared this winter, figuring that way I couldn't be framed for any of their dirty deals. The backup copies are at my apartment on the Upper East Side, but I don't know if it's safe to go back there yet."

"So you weren't sure who to trust." Finally, Vanessa began to understand Alec's need to slip into hiding. "You had reason to suspect your partners were making an alliance with your uncle behind your back."

"And if I find out they've been cooking the books, I'm going to blow the whistle on both their asses and get them out of the business for good." He rubbed a weary hand across his face. "I'm tired of always having to watch my back just to do my job. I can do more good at the rec center and probably be a hell of a lot safer, too."

Vanessa didn't blame him for putting some safety measures in place. But even with stepped-up security, she didn't plan to set foot in the Bronx again any time soon. She could untangle the rest of Alec Messina's convoluted problems from the safety of Manhattan.

Or so she really, really hoped. Bottom line, she'd do whatever necessary to nail the guys who'd held a gun on her last night and resurrected her nightmares.

"Care to tell me how you struck up such a close relationship with your uncle's mistress?" She hadn't meant to ask the question. It just slipped out while her eyes locked on the closing lines of one of the e-mails.

"Are you asking as a cop or as the woman I slept with last night?" Alec didn't pull any punches. Even when she had a carjacking to investigate, Alec's abundance of shady friends to wade through and a mob mistress with her claws on the man Vanessa had gone to bed with.

Not exactly a red-letter day.

"I'm asking because I damn well want to know."
She hadn't planned to quiz Alec about the women in his
life, but what choice did she have when he waved this
female under her nose? "The writer of this e-mail makes
it plain as day that her…sex…is yours for the taking.
Did you take her up on the offer?"

Snatching the file folder from Vanessa's grip, Alec
flung it on the sofa nearby.

"Hell no." He laid an arm across her shoulders, his
hand winding its way into her hair as if to hold her in
place by the long length. "Hasn't anyone wholly inappropriate ever come on to you before, whether you were
looking for a connection or not?"

She met his dark gaze, experiencing the electricity
that sparked back and forth between them, a ripple of
energy that increased with every breath she took.

Didn't matter that she was pissed at the idea of Alec
possibly sleeping with another woman. If anything, the
edge of frustration only heightened the heat.

"I meet some very inappropriate people in my line
of work." Of course, she only had one man in mind at
the moment. Someone she never should have looked at,
let alone touched. She seemed to have lost all common
sense where he was concerned, although she had to
admit she didn't miss common sense when she had a
hefty dose of sexual healing to make up for the loss.

"I'll bet you do." He twisted his hand fractionally
tighter in the strands, enough to steer her closer. "But

just because you get propositioned doesn't mean you jump into bed with anyone."

"Right. Normally." She'd brought razor-sharp focus to her work for the past four and a half years because of it. But now? The edges around this whole case were starting to blur. "Last night being a notable exception."

"You still think I'm someone inappropriate?" His hold on her hair loosened as he slid back a few inches. "Hell, Vanessa. You wouldn't have got anywhere near me if you really believed I had a hand in any of the charges my partners are trying to stick on me."

She was glad he thought so because she didn't trust herself to know anything anymore. The carjacking had put her through the wringer and spit her out a little more vulnerable. A whole lot more tense.

"Maybe. But I'd feel better about spending the night with you if this case was behind me and I didn't have the guilt of secret knowledge to carry around. I'm not going to look my lieutenant in the eye and tell him I couldn't find Alec Messina."

"Maybe by the time you see him again, you'll be able to tell the truth."

She didn't answer, knowing he wouldn't want to hear about her plan to contact the precinct today. But how could she help Alec without accessing the combined strength of NYPD resources and her partner's clear cop-vision? Wes Shaw was a detective she respected because he possessed brains and balls in equal doses, but opted to rely on street smarts rather than guts ninety percent of the time, which seemed damn rare in a lot of cops. He'd have good advice for what Vanessa should do next, and more importantly, he could make inquiries about the carjackers.

Judging by Alec's quiet expletive, however, Vanessa figured he'd already guessed her plan.

"You can't go into work today, Vanessa. We've been over this."

"We could find out who took your car." The nerdy researcher inside her couldn't wait to access the computer at her desk. "For that matter, if I don't call into work and tell them something, my partner is going to have half the precinct out looking for me since I've never skipped a day on the job."

No question, Wes would be worried. His last partner had died while working undercover, so she wouldn't give him any reason to be uneasy about her. They had always been content to give one another a lot of room, but even laid-back Wes would protest if he discovered the extent of her plan to hide out with Alec until she could ensure his safety.

"You're working on a perfect attendance record?" A small, rare smile caught her off guard.

"I made a commitment to this job." For reasons that still scared the hell out of her. "I didn't sign on with the police department to tick off personal days and let somebody else solve my cases. I took it because I wanted to…"

Nail the bastards who hurt Gena.

"Protect and serve?"

"Something like that." She just hoped she hadn't lost her edge by sleeping with Alec and turning on all the emotions she'd managed to shut off. In the past, she'd dealt with a lot of scary crap by being detached. Remote.

Now she was practically choking on new sensations bombarding her from every angle. Fear? Definitely.

Lust? Even more prominent than fear. Especially since Alec had never bothered to button his shirt.

Damn, but she'd never make her call to Wes if she didn't get her mind back on her case and off Alec's body.

SHE DIDN'T EVEN CHECK OUT his package.

Alec had no idea what to make of this woman who took her job so damn seriously she never called in sick, yet she seemed to have all the time in the world to think about sex. Or maybe she just devoted a lot of time to making *him* think about sex. Either way, he was stuck battling big-time attraction and the most persistent freaking hard-on in the known universe.

"So contact your partner." He could see her point about not wanting the guy to worry needlessly and maybe draw a lot of attention to the fact she was gone. "But I wouldn't use the apartment phone in case they track their incoming calls."

"I've got my cell phone." She didn't reach for it, however. She just stared up at him with that endless confidence he'd seen in her before anything else yesterday.

And what did it say about him that the snooty tilt of this woman's nose turned him on?

"I'm not too keen on this call in the first place, lady, so if you want to dial those numbers anytime soon I suggest you get on it before I wrestle you to the ground and have you every which way I want you." He ground his teeth to keep himself from touching her, grinding himself into her.

"In your dreams, I'm sure you could." Smiling her Mona Lisa grin she flipped open her phone and turned her back on him to touch base with her partner.

He placated himself by making plans to tear her clothes off the moment she finished her conversation. Hell, maybe wrestling her to the ground wasn't such a bad idea.

"Wes? Are you alone?" Vanessa's soft words for her partner on the other end of the phone yanked him back to the present.

Her body language shifted. Even standing behind her Alec could see a tension hum through her shoulders as she spoke to the guy—some noble cop crusader who was more her type than a wanted man. Alec acknowledged that it made him a caveman to wonder if she slept with this tool of a guy, but he found himself thinking it anyhow.

"I can't come in today, and I won't be in for a few days. You think you can let the department know? Tell them I decided to cash in on some personal time at the last minute?" She walked as she talked, putting space between her and Alec, which he damn well didn't appreciate.

Still, knowing he should give her some privacy to talk didn't make his feet move away. Instead, he continued to watch her walk and talk, her movements slightly clipped as if she were agitated. Or as if she were lying.

"I don't want to talk to Russell. It's sort of complicated and I can't really get into it now, but I need a favor." Her tone turned soft again, reminding Alec how easily a woman could wrap a man around her finger. Donata had done it with him, convincing him she needed help as she drew him deeper and deeper into dangerous waters with his uncle.

Vanessa would never be like that though. Would she? She seemed too self-sufficient—too proud—to play those kinds of games.

He flipped through the news stations on TV again, but kept the sound muted as he half watched for updates on the recent string of drug busts and listened to Vanessa's conversation.

"I need some information on a carjacking last night. A couple of guys in the Bronx rolled a Mercedes sedan and I'd appreciate any news on the whereabouts of this car, but I need to keep it on the low." She went on to give the license plate over the phone along with the address of the incident, but repeatedly dodged any other details.

After listening to her go back and forth with the partner who was apparently getting annoyed about the whole secrecy thing, Alec watched Vanessa drop down into a chair in the dining room, her movements brittle.

Who the hell did her partner think he was to upset her like that? Alec considered yanking the phone out of her hand to tell the guy where he could step off.

Vanessa nodded at something the guy on the other end was saying. "I appreciate what you've been through in the past, but this is totally different. I'm going to level with you about the whole thing as soon as I can but I can't risk jeopardizing something—" her eyes flitted over to Alec "—or someone."

Alec jerked his gaze back to the television, pissed off at having been caught eavesdropping. He wasn't sure which bugged him more—his stupid jealousy she might have slept with her do-gooder cop partner, or this restless unease that flared up at the notion she might care enough about Alec to worry about him.

Stabbing buttons mindlessly on the remote, he told himself that he was just another case to her. She'd put that into perspective for him damn quick this morning. In her eyes, Alec had been relegated to a wanted-man-turned-carjacking-victim she could save. She was the do-gooder type, too, right?

He hadn't realized she'd sewn up her conversation until she appeared in his line of vision, her sleek curves obscuring an idiotic commercial on TV.

"He won't cover for me for long." She folded her arms beneath subtle cleavage he wanted to reacquaint himself with as soon as possible. "I need to get back to work within a couple of days or he'll start making waves."

Alec nodded, even though he scarcely heard what she was saying. He might have missed out on the rest of her phone conversation, but he hadn't forgotten his plans for her as soon as it was done. Besides, she didn't seem like such a damn do-gooder when she was underneath him, screaming his name while he came inside her.

So what if she thought he needed saving? He needed the taste of her again.

"Are you listening to me?" Frustration laced her words, her fingers squeezing the phone in a death grip. "We don't have much time to figure out who's trying to frame you with the embezzlement charges, or if your uncle wants you dead." She paced in his line of sight, her restless body a hell of a lot more entertaining than anything he might have found via satellite. "Which reminds me of something else I thought of this morning. If your uncle found your hiding place and put those carjackers in our path last night, why wouldn't he have just had you killed then?"

Damn. She didn't make it easy to keep his focus on sex. Maybe he just needed to shift *her* focus.

"My uncle doesn't want me dead yet." Flipping aside the remote, he rose to his feet, ready to claim what he'd been wanting all morning. "Dead men don't pay."

"I thought you said you weren't giving kickbacks to

your uncle?" She stilled, her thoughts way too far off the sexual path for his comfort.

Stalking closer to her, he paused a few inches away, breathing in the morning clean scent of her.

"I'm not." He eased her phone from her grasp and tossed it on the couch with his remote. "But organized crime makes a profit off of guys they get over a barrel. And Sergio thinks he's putting me over one with pressure from my partners and pressure from his mistress. He doesn't understand how determined I am that the bastard will never see one red cent of my money."

She drew in a sharp breath, possibly because he tugged her closer by the hem of her shirt. His shirt. He watched the rapid pulse of a jumpy little vein at her neck, convinced he could almost see her breath.

In.

Out.

"If you're trying to convince me you're moving on the right side of the law, you probably shouldn't drag me around by the shirttails." Her breathy voice gripped him by the gonads, making him hot and hard and hungry as hell.

"Yeah?" He dug beneath her shirt to palm her bare back, soaking up the feel of cool, smooth skin through his fingertips. "If you're trying to convince me you're such a concerned cop, you ought to quit looking at me like you want to get me naked and have me for breakfast."

"Oh, please." She rolled her eyes and tried to twist

out of his grip, but the leftover tension from her phone conversation eased away as he smoothed his palm up one shoulder blade and down the other. "I wasn't even glancing in your direction."

"Are you kidding?" He flicked one bra strap off her shoulder. "You practically incinerated me where I sat. I'm pretty sure the couch is still smoking."

Apparently she didn't think much of his delivery because she shoved away from him a little harder this time. Only he held on tighter.

Just out of curiosity's sake.

"You're one really messed-up guy, you know that?" She dropped downward suddenly in a boneless heap, a tricky self-defense move that made it tough to hold on to her.

His admiration for her only kicked up a little higher. Damn, but she was a dynamo.

"I never denied it." He fell on her before she could scramble away, being careful not to put his full weight on her as he pinned her to the floor for the second time in less than twenty-four hours. And he could appreciate that his enjoyment of the position probably did make him a messed-up guy. "But what do you think it says about you that you're breathing even harder than me right now?"

Her breasts pressed softly against his chest with every sweet inhalation, the friction making blood rush to his groin. Damn well made him dizzy.

"Are you suggesting I need to work on my conditioning?" A slender sable eyebrow arched with the question as she finally grew still.

"Wiseass." He lowered his lips to hers, unable to wait even five more seconds to have the taste of her on his tongue. He pulled back after just one lick, knowing he wouldn't be able to speak coherently in another minute. "Your conditioning is oh-so-freaking fine, but I think you need to work on a few other things. I'm going to consider it my sworn duty to make sure you get plenty of practice."

8

VANESSA HAD NEVER DONE any undercover work before, but she suspected the sensation of assuming another identity would feel something like this.

As her arms slid up his back to twine around Alec, she recognized her behavior seemed foreign. Out of character. She'd never been the kind of woman to fall into bed with a man and then engage in nonstop sexual fantasies with him.

Correction. She'd dragged men to her bed before in those horrible, dark months after her sister's accident in an attempt to lose herself. But there'd always been a certain detachment from those encounters that had been more about escaping pain than finding pleasure.

With Alec, the pleasure swelled so high it threatened to wash away everything else around her. And after last night's brush with mortality in the form of a gun planted to her head, Vanessa welcomed this fiery cleansing, the intense heat that burned away everything inside her but pure sensation.

Even while kissing they grappled for control, Vanessa pushing against his shoulders while he kept up a steady pressure on her legs to keep her still. She'd never played those kinds of games with a man before, her sexual experience frighteningly limited even with the handful of guys she'd coldly roped into one-night stands. She barely remembered those weeks of guilt and recrimination after Gena's accident anyhow.

Thank God.

"Is this the same vice grip you use on unsuspecting crooks?" Alec muttered the words between kisses, voice just a little strangled.

"Sorry." Loosening her grip around his chest, she smoothed the rippled muscles up his sides, savoring the tapered lines of a strong upper body down to lean hips. "Actually, I make it a point not to let the criminal element get too close to me if I can help it."

He arched back from her to meet her eyes. "Yeah? I'm feeling pretty damn flattered then."

The warm sincerity of those simple words scared her, reminded her she couldn't afford to get emotionally involved with this man who had already commanded every shred of her sexual attention.

"You're going to be feeling a whole lot more than that in a minute." Diverting his attention proved easy and oh so rewarding as she walked her fingers down his hip to the front of his fly.

His eyes closed, head falling down to rest on hers as she skimmed her palm between their bodies to cradle his erection. The showered-clean scent of him matched her own just-bathed fragrance, but he still smelled different. Spicy and musky. Deliciously male.

He tensed with her touch, as if he wouldn't allow himself simply to enjoy the stroke of her fingers up and down the length of him. His thigh slid in between hers, chasing away her questing palm as he pressed up against the hot center of her sheathed only by her jeans.

Her first inclination was simply to open for him, to ease her legs farther apart to welcome the hard strength of him. But in the hard light of day, sprawled out on this anonymous living room floor with a man she'd known less than a day, that seemed unbelievably intimate. True, she couldn't deny herself another chance to test the raw sexual firepower of Alec Messina, but she didn't have to wantonly indulge her every hedonistic whim. Instead, she used that shifting of his thigh on top of her to take advantage of his diverted attention.

Sucking in a breath, she braced her arms against his shoulders and gently shoved, rolling them onto Alec's back so she could gain the top position.

"Victory." She whispered her triumph in his ear as she whipped off the tank shirt and tossed it in the general direction of the couch.

"Don't worry, the view from down here is going a long way toward soothing my ego." He reached up to tug apart the clasp on the front of her bra, making the two cups fall away.

Leaving her naked to the waist.

A sense of empowerment slid over her, although she

wasn't sure if that was because she straddled a gorgeous man or because she'd effectively wrestled him to his back. Probably a little of both.

She might have savored her victorious position a little longer if Alec hadn't crunched his abs enough to rise up to a half-sitting position, putting his mouth right at breast level and giving her an eyeful of a ripped six-pack. And then his mouth closed over one taut pink nipple and she couldn't think anymore. Liquid heat suffused her limbs as he laved her breasts with moist stabs of his tongue.

Her hair swung down past her shoulders, sliding over her breasts to brush against his cheek as he kissed her. Vanessa found her fingers spearing into his hair, too, automatically flexing against his scalp to keep the pleasurable pressure against her cleavage.

She forgot all about her need to be on top, her ever-vigilant inner warrioress gladly taking a step back long enough to enjoy Alec's clever mouth. Perhaps he sensed her weakening commitment to the upper position because he rolled her back to the floor, his arm covering the abraded skin on her spine from the carpet. The knowledge that he remembered those small hurts and thought to protect them reminded her she needed to pull back, protect *herself* before she started caring about a man with undeniable ties to crime—whether he wanted them or not.

But knowing all of that didn't stop her wrapping her leg around his, lifting her hips up to his in wanton offering. She needed this joining, this red-hot completion just one more time before she forced herself back on the straight and narrow later. Tomorrow. She'd been too emotionally wasted last night to fully appreciate the nuances of sex with Alec, a mistake she wouldn't make twice.

Dragging her eyes open she stared up at the mysterious stranger kissing her, sliding off her clothes to bare herself. His coal-dark lashes fanned out on stark cheekbones, his face hewn with harsh lines and framed by silky brown hair cut close to his head.

Perhaps sensing her stare, he opened his eyes to meet her gaze, his whole body humming with the same tension that wound through her. She skimmed her hand over his chest, absorbing the rapid beat of his heart.

"I'll never be able to get naked if you don't let go of me," he finally whispered to her, gently slipping his hand underneath her thigh.

Sure enough, she still had her leg wound around his, pressing him more tightly to her. Damn, she was needy when it came to Alec, her body conspiring against her to keep him right next to her.

"Just trying to get my workout." Relaxing her calf muscles, she eased off, freeing him.

Praying he wouldn't go far.

"A workout?" Levering himself up from the floor, Alec stood to shed his pants. Boxers. And she'd thought he looked good in the dark? Lord have mercy. The sculpted strength of him and imposing presence could make the most detached woman swoon. "Be careful what you wish for, lady. You just might get it."

Before she could contemplate what that might mean, he bent down to pull her to her feet and then half steered, half kissed her backward across the floor. She would have stumbled over her own toes if he hadn't been there to guide her safely. The kiss, the man, the return of five years' worth of pent-up emotions combined to knock her on her ass.

No wait, the force of Alec pushing her down to the couch knocked her on her butt. She suspected he had other plans for her, but she couldn't help but notice her position put her eye level with his cock. And since when did she waste prime opportunities?

She'd never had a chance to develop much of a technique in this arena with all of her doomed sexual experiments. But Alec's prime male specimen gave her major new inspiration.

Time to lose herself in sex.

ALEC HADN'T MEANT TO IMPLY he wanted…that.

But hell, what man wouldn't be tempted once he spied a woman's mouth so close to his member? Especially since Vanessa stared at him like his cock was an all new treat, an ice-cream cone waiting for a lick.

An extra large ice-cream cone.

Possibly his irreverent thoughts kept him standing there a little too long. Or maybe it was the way Vanessa caressed him with her eyes. Still, he hadn't meant to suggest she take him deep into her mouth and stroke her tongue over every inch of him.

But who was he to tell her that she shouldn't?

Heat blasted through his veins, burning away intelligent thought until nothing remained but her warm, wet mouth and a pleasure so deep, so all-consuming he counted himself about five seconds away from losing it.

"Wait." He wanted to get inside her again. Take her places no other guy had.

Four...

But she didn't show any signs of stopping. Instead, she hummed a little sigh of pleasure while she licked him, the vibration of the sound making his eyes cross and his knees damn near buckle.

Three seconds...

He forced himself to scramble back, his brain barely functioning but still he knew he wanted a full-out connection with Vanessa before their time together disappeared. He didn't know what exactly he wanted from her, but some basic function of male ego urged him to make as much of a lasting impression on her body and mind as she had on him.

"What?" She looked dazed for a second, worried maybe, that he'd stopped her.

Could that be right? She seemed too damn self-assured ever to harbor those kinds of insecurities.

Unequipped to think right now, Alec settled for finding the condom he'd stashed when he'd dressed earlier.

He rolled it on as he covered her, drawing her down to lie on the couch with him.

"I just want to get inside you." He pushed her thighs apart, fingers taking sweet liberties with the slick heat he found there. "Make you remember me long after you're safe and sound in your police precinct again."

He wrested a long moan from her lips as he edged two fingers deep inside her. She was incredibly hot. Tight.

"I think I'll—" a gasp cut her words apart as he crooked his finger forward to massage her deep inside "—remember."

He could have taken her over the edge with just a little more pressure. A little more angle of his finger, maybe. But selfishly, he wanted them to hurtle into that sexual abyss together, to reach completion when he was buried to the hilt in her.

Molding his mouth to hers he kissed her, teased her, kept her on that pleasure precipice as he entered her. Slowly. Fully.

Vanessa arched beneath him, her limber body determined to torment him. He wanted to control this moment, to draw out the pleasure for both of them. But her hips wouldn't rest, her abs crunching as she lifted herself with him, making it impossible for him to withdraw. Her hold on him tightened, pulsed with wet heat. Alec knew he didn't stand a chance of holding back, not with her squeezing him, enveloping him until he had no choice but to lose himself.

He drove into her, gripping her with a fierceness he couldn't keep at bay any longer. Later he'd figure out what it was about Vanessa that called him to put his guard down, to sacrifice a small sliver of control. In his world that kind of lapse could have dangerous consequences, possibly fatal. Whatever was happening between them, Alec needed it to stop. Soon.

Right after he recovered from sex that wrung him dry, robbing him of the most rudimentary thinking capabilities.

He just hoped Vanessa understood. Because even though he needed to distance himself from her to stay focused on keeping them both safe, instinct told him she wasn't the sort of woman who would take kindly to the notion of being protected.

A FEW HOURS LATER, Vanessa awoke to the chime of her cell phone. The noise startled her, making her realize late-morning quickies messed with her natural biorhythms and threw her off her schedule. Either that, or late-night carjackings took a toll on a woman.

Scrambling over the sheets, she reached for the phone and realized she'd left it in the living room, before Alec had carried her in here as though she were some kind of medieval maiden.

As if.

"I don't know if you should answer it." Alec appeared in the doorway, phone in hand as he studied the caller ID window. "What if they're trying to track you?"

Vanessa snagged the ringing phone and saw Wes's cell number on the display.

"Not a chance." She pressed the answer button, trusting her partner completely. Wes might give her a hard time about keeping her location secret, but he'd never try to find her without letting her know first. She didn't waste any time cutting to the chase with him. "You find out anything?"

Self-conscious about talking to Wes while naked, especially since Alec's eyes burned into her with frank possessiveness, Vanessa yanked the covers up to her chin.

"Some guys showed up at a bar on Tremont Street last night with cash to spare and talking smack about landing a primo car," Wes said. "The local cops haven't done squat about it yet because the Raven Club falls on the line between precincts and—"

"And no one ever thinks it's their territory. Trust me, I know the place." The worst crap always went down there. "It's totally lawless. The Wild West of the South Bronx."

"You can't go there alone, Vanessa." Wes's tone meant no argument allowed—something pretty rare for her loner partner who appreciated their loose collaboration as much as she did. "And judging by the plate number I ran, I have a damn good idea who you're with. Are you sure you know what you're getting into?"

"Don't worry about it." Vanessa's eyes flicked over Alec as she wondered what Wes thought of her joining forces with a guy whose allegiance to the law was questionable at best. She had no doubt he could hold his own at the borough's most notorious bar, however. If anything, his bad-guy reputation would probably help them. "I'm not going alone."

She disconnected before Wes could argue. The last thing she wanted to do right now was try defending Alec to a detective, not when she hadn't really gotten a handle on him herself. She trusted Alec on a gut level she couldn't quite explain. But even to her own ears, that sounded like a flimsy justification.

"You found out something." Alec's stare remained hard and inscrutable, nothing like the hot looks he'd just been giving her.

"The guys who took the car went barhopping to brag afterward." The thought pissed her off more than she cared to admit. "Or at least, some guys were talking up a big score at the Raven Club. My guess is your Mercedes was the prize in question."

"You're not going to the Raven." He didn't even blink at the news they might be able to find the carjackers.

"Actually, I am." She'd be damned if he would pull some archaic he-man rescue BS with her. "And I'm counting on you to back me up."

"The place is a powder keg on a good night." He leaned a shoulder into the door frame, not even bothering to enter the room to have an argument with her. "And when confrontational cops show up asking questions, the whole bar can erupt with violence. All the craziest bastards in town hang out there, just waiting for an excuse to go ballistic."

"I grew up in the Bronx." The Torres sisters carried the physical and emotional scars to prove it. "I know better than to stir up trouble in that kind of no-man's-land. I'm a professional, remember?"

He stayed silent so long she debated launching another argument. What she wanted to do was get up and get dressed, but somehow it seemed too awkward to stomp around the room naked while she recovered all her clothes.

"I lost my gun in the carjacking."

After all that silence, that's what he came up with?

"So use another one." She would remain calm. Reasonable. Talk her way around his worries. "I promise I won't ask you to show a license or anything, okay? I just need you to cover me in there or else I'll have to get my partner involved and I thought you didn't want—"

He cursed in at least two languages, one of which she recognized as Spanish since her Nana had used those words often enough. As for the other, she guessed maybe Italian.

Surprised at the outpouring of frustration from a guy who seemed extremely controlled, Vanessa waited. Letting him vent.

"Shit."

Make that three languages.

When he was finally done, he moved quietly into the room to sit on the edge of the bed.

"I respect that you're a cop and you do this kind of thing for a living." He laid his hand on her knee through the layers of white bed linens. "But someone wants me dead, Vanessa. I can't afford for you to get wrapped up in that because that's my problem, not yours."

She hadn't been prepared for him to speak that bluntly. But the sheen of urgency in his eyes reinforced his words.

"You're trying to keep me safe." She turned over the idea in her mind, identifying with the need to protect someone. Still, she wasn't any anonymous someone. She'd been certified lethal in kendo, her fighting style of choice. And when they went to the Raven Club, she'd be packing a weapon. "Tell me this, Alec. Did you really have any evidence to show me last night, or did you just make up the whole tale about the accounting disks to be sure I didn't leave the rec center alone?"

Suspicion turned her skin cold, her leg tensing beneath his touch. What if she'd slept with someone who'd played her for a fool?

"No." He squeezed her knee as if he could impress the answer on her. "Hell no. We could go to my real apartment right now to retrieve other copies of the disks, but returning to any of my old haunts is risky."

Logically, she understood his point. Still, the cop in her couldn't help be suspicious. Wary. Sure she trusted him enough to come home with him last night. But that was because he'd risked his own neck to stay with her when the carjackers had dragged her out the Mercedes's door. He could have floored the gas then and there and left her to her own devices, but he'd stayed.

The very incident that made her trust him then, made her leery now. What other lengths would he go to in order to keep her safe?

Would he lie to her?

"Risky or not, I need to see the evidence if I'm going to jeopardize my neck and my professional reputation to help you." She knew it wouldn't be easy to give him that kind of ultimatum, but she hadn't been prepared for the sharp sting of loss she felt when his hand moved away from her knee.

"And if somebody's watching my apartment building?"

"You've been in hiding for months. Do you really think your defection is so important to your uncle that he could spare enough manpower to put your apartment on full-time surveillance?"

"More likely he's paying off someone in the building to keep an eye on my door."

"Then all we need to do is make sure that person doesn't see us." Clutching the sheet to her breasts, Vanessa mourned the absence of the rapport they'd shared last night. The touches. Still, she'd never help Alec out of this mess if she didn't start doing what she did best— the cold, hard investigating.

"If I agree to secure the disks for you, then you can

at least let me ask the questions at the bar." Rising off the bed, he stalked toward the door. "Fair enough?"

"Hardly." She wouldn't give him an inch on this or he'd think he could call all the shots. "We work together to get into the apartment and then it's another team effort at the club to find out who hauled me out of your car by my earlobe. You can't turn this into your show after you convinced me to help you."

Pausing in the door to the living room, he seemed to consider her words.

"Fine." He held up his hands in surrender, giving in too easily and making her suspicious all over again. "We go together."

"No arguments?"

His eyes narrowed as his gaze swept over her. "I make it a habit not to argue with naked women."

"Really? Well I have no intention of ripping my clothes off every time I need you to back me up, so forget it." She reached for her shirt on the floor beside the bed. "I'll be ready to go in five minutes. Why don't you start thinking about how we're going to get into the building without anyone seeing you?"

"We need a distraction." He didn't seem in any hurry to leave as he reached behind a picture frame on the wall to reveal a small metal safe.

More secrets. More surprises from Alec.

"A distraction makes sense." She scooped up her bra and slid into the straps as she watched him dial the safe combination, his back to her.

"And as I watch your reflection in this mildly shiny metallic surface, it occurs to me that it would be a hell of a distraction if we send a stripper to the doorman."

"Very original." She made an obscene gesture in the direction of the safe, where he watched her, then finished dressing as he pried open the vault. No sense being sly now.

The unmistakable click of a gun being loaded made her forget all about zipping her pants.

Looking up, she found Alec checking the safety on a .357. A lean, mean weapon very capable of backing her up at the Raven Club or anywhere else they went in the pursuit of justice today. What might have happened if Alec Messina had been on the corner of 172nd Street with her five years ago?

"If you've got a better idea how to create a distraction, I'm all ears." He tucked the .357 into his belt to rest at his hip. Right where a jacket would cover it.

His ease with the weapon concerned her even as it comforted.

"As a matter of fact I do." She figured this was the perfect time for her to roll out a few of her less orthodox ideas for battling crime. After her past and her present had collided in a night from hell yesterday, she didn't have any intention of solving this one by the book. "And it doesn't involve any strippers or guns."

9

TWO HOURS LATER, Alec stepped onto the elevator in his deserted apartment building and stared at Vanessa through the eyeholes of some kind of gas-mask contraption that looked straight out of a fifties horror flick.

Attack of the Insect Men from Outer Space.

Vanessa had picked up the space-age–looking gear from the trunk of her car when they'd stopped at her parking garage on the Lower West Side. She'd convinced him to pretend to be part of a bomb squad while she flashed her badge at the desk clerk to gain them entry into his apartment without any witnesses.

Now, she joined him in the elevator and pushed the button for the seventh floor. His floor.

"You're freaking brilliant." The doors closed, but he didn't remove his mask yet in case the building kept security cameras in the elevators. "You sure your department won't boot you out for saying there was a bomb threat in the building?"

As the car chimed its arrival on seven, the doors swept open onto an empty hallway where he led her to his apartment.

"If the desk clerk is taking money from the mob to keep an eye out for you, I refuse to care how we gained safe passage in here." She whipped off her mask once he opened the door and ushered her inside the space he hadn't laid eyes on in six months. "Besides, I convinced the hot-pretzel vendor out front to offer a half-off special for the next half hour. There's only a handful of people home at this time of day anyway, and with cheap pretzels, how can anyone complain?"

Alec took off his mask, too, and set it aside until he could collect his backup copy of the accounting records. The *clean* accounting records before someone had revised them to make it look as though he'd been pilfering out more than his fair share.

"If I've learned one thing in life, it's that someone always complains." He made a visual inspection of the apartment, moving quickly since Vanessa hoped to be out of the building within twenty minutes. "Help yourself to whatever you'd like, but let's be careful not to displace any of the dust. I'd rather keep it looking like we were never in here in case any unwanted company comes calling."

"I'm fine." Vanessa's suit crinkled as she walked, following him through the short corridor leading to the two bedrooms and a den in back. "Want me to help you with anything? Pack more clothes? Dig up any more hidden weapons?"

"Again with the guns." He slid open the closet in the den and removed a ceiling tile just above a set of storage shelves, wishing she'd forget about seeing the .357. She'd mentioned it twice on their drive uptown. "You know, I don't ask you about why you happen to have gas masks in your car trunk."

"They're exterminator suits." She plucked at the Mylar-looking fibers of the shirt she'd draped over her outfit while she watched him fish around the ductwork in the ceiling opening. "My sister is a lawyer, and she's dating an exterminator one of her partners represented last winter."

Finally, he found what he sought—a padded envelope wrapped in insulation like the other ductwork. Not exactly a high-tech disguise, but he'd hoped it would blend in enough with the surroundings to go unnoticed by anyone who decided to fish around up there.

"An exterminator?" He tore off the insulation and tucked the envelope under his arm before replacing the tile. "Seems like an odd match for an attorney."

"No worse than a cop and the guy with mob ties." She picked up a few stray strands of the insulation and tucked them in her pocket. "You found what you need?"

"Assuming the disks survived the fluctuations in climate up there—yes." He didn't need anything else from the apartment that had served as little more than a place to crash between jobs. He'd spent most of his time on job sites for McPherson Real Estate the past three years. "Let's put on the bug masks and get the hell out of here before someone decides to check into the identity of their bomb experts more closely."

He walked slowly through the room, careful not to raise any dust as he headed for the living room.

Until he noticed Vanessa wasn't following him.

"You coming?" He turned to see her still in the den, staring at something on his desk.

"How long did you say it's been since you were here?" Gently, she flipped over a page of his desk calendar.

"Six months, give or take." He picked up the bulky masks they'd worn in and retraced his steps toward the den, eager to be on their way now that they'd retrieved the disks. "Why?"

"You've had the evidence to prove your innocence all that time and you never came forward?" Her fingers fell away from the calendar as she straightened, but she didn't move toward the door. Instead she seemed rooted to the spot as she stared at him.

Measuring his words, he had the niggling feeling he was missing something here and couldn't quite grasp the link.

"The police were never involved until recently. Why come forward? Whoever is trying to set me up has a lot of money at stake and possible criminal charges hanging over their heads. My gut says that person isn't going to let me anywhere near the cops without retaliation of some sort."

"So you just hid the evidence and opened a rec center while you waited for…what?" The skepticism in her tone suggested she thought he was off his rocker.

"For the smoke to clear." Hell, these were details he didn't want to delve into. Especially not with a woman who'd gotten under his skin the way she had in the past twenty hours. "For my enemies to be made known. Can't we talk about it in the car?"

He nudged her arm with her mask, ready to make tracks from this lifeless apartment.

"Hell yes, we can talk about it in the car." The inscrutable expression on her face transformed to obvious anger. "Right after we finish talking about this part of it here. Because I want to know if you've ever considered that by keeping your evidence and your secrets to yourself, you are actually protecting a felon."

"I told you—I've been waiting for somebody to make a false move. Reveal themselves." He stepped over to the window and edged aside the blinds enough to see down to the street. The handful of evacuated tenants seemed to be keeping the pretzel vendor busy while the building superintendent scowled and talked into his cell phone off to one side of the crowd.

Instincts hummed to life, urging him to get out now.

"If nobody ever comes forward with information, the police are left with a damn big burden to piece together information at a crime scene they didn't personally witness." Her voice quieted, her flash of anger transforming to a bitterness he didn't understand. "Maybe if you were willing to share your evidence with the police six months ago, they could have used it in conjunction with their own information to make arrests and serve some justice."

"Or maybe they would have considered the source and assumed any guy related to Sergio Alteri must be part of a crime family." She wasn't naive enough to think he could have just strolled into a cop shop with his disks under his arm and be taken at his word. Was she?

He moved to lower the blind when a police car came into view down on the street below. Slowing, the vehicle came to a full stop when the building superintendent flagged it down.

Time to get the hell out of Dodge.

"Police are here." Shoving the headgear on Vanessa, he slid on his own and lunged for the door. "We can take a back exit if we hurry."

He didn't need to hear her agree. She launched into action as fast as him, tugging the door shut behind them as they moved into the corridor.

By silent agreement they took the stairs down. Seven floors flew by as they hustled toward street level, the computer disks a reassuring weight in his inside pocket as they smacked against his chest. When they reached the final door to the sunny late afternoon, Alec levered it open and walked briskly toward her car parked a half block down the street.

He kept his mask on to help protect his identity from his neighbors or anyone else inclined to sell him out to the first person who showed up looking for him. The pseudo bomb-squad outfit attracted plenty of attention, however, including a few shouts for information from building tenants who'd wandered around to the other side of the building.

Vanessa picked up the pace the last few steps, sprinting the rest of the way to her car and vaulting inside. She had the engine in gear and the vehicle in motion before he'd completely shut the passenger-side door.

Alec peered into the rearview mirror as she sped away on the relatively quiet side street.

"Only a couple of gawkers saw us leave." He tossed the exterminator mask into her back seat. "Maybe we should ditch the car in case they do a check on the plates."

"This is New York, remember?" Vanessa shook out her long, dark hair from the confines of the headgear as they turned a corner. "No one ever turns in any information to help the police."

Her darkly muttered words called to mind her anger back in his apartment.

"Okay, what gives with all the righteous indignation about submitting evidence?" He settled back into the seat, as she drove uptown toward the Third Avenue Bridge.

The Bronx.

Somehow her unease with the city's toughest borough came into play here. She'd admitted to being uncomfortable there last night, despite her thorough martial art training and the fact that she carried a weapon. Now today she was getting more on edge with every passing streetlight.

When she didn't say anything for the long moments they waited for an out-of-towner to figure out how to get around a double-parked delivery truck, Alec knew he'd hit on something.

"This thing—whatever is making you gung ho about submitting evidence—it has something to do with why you hate the Bronx, doesn't it?"

A CHORUS OF HORNS BLARED at the tourist backing up and pulling forward. Vanessa half wished she could join in the cacophony of frustration. Pound her fist on the steering wheel for good measure.

She couldn't deny Alec's observation.

"Why don't you leave the investigating to me, hot-shot?" Wheeling the car around the perplexed tourist who patiently waited to be let into traffic with his blinker flashing, Vanessa maneuvered up Third Avenue and told herself she would not break a sweat in front of the man watching her like a hawk from the passenger seat.

Still, her neck went hot, her pulse pounding with an urgency unusual for her. She'd been called an ice queen more than once around the precinct, and not just because she'd turned down plenty of offers from the guys on the force. She had a reputation for being in control. Cool under pressure.

And yet right now, she seemed to be fracturing at the seams at a question she ought to be able to blow off.

"Vanessa?" Alec reached over the console from the

passenger seat to lay a hand beside hers on the wheel. Not taking control, but suggesting it without much subtlety. From his raised voice, she got the impression he might have called her name more than once. "Let me drive."

"Shit." She hadn't realized until he suggested it that she was hanging on by a thread. Old symptoms from five years ago—the flashes of heat, the sudden wash of fear—reared up in small doses. How the hell had that happened? "Okay. I think the close call at the apartment building caught me off guard."

Lame excuse. She knew it. She knew he knew it. But if she didn't start reasserting some control for herself, she didn't know what might happen. No sense ramming her car into a fire hydrant because she was warding off a panic attack.

"There's a dock by the river up here. Under the bridge." He pointed to a turnoff, a side street safely on the Manhattan side of the Third Avenue Bridge. East Harlem she could handle.

Pulling out of traffic, she didn't bother getting close to the dock where a few power-company trucks blocked the way. There was a gap in the parked cars to one side of the street and with no problem she pulled into the vacant space behind a motorcycle.

Finding something intelligent to say to Alec that would make him drop the whole incident—including his question about why the Bronx made her spaz out—now *that* presented a problem.

Hoping maybe just to blow it off instead, she breezed out of the car and headed around to the passenger side. He held the door for her while she slid into the seat, accepting her sidekick position as if it weren't a huge slap to her ego.

She attempted to stretch her mouth into a smile, but that might have been a mistake, since her effort only earned her a scowl as he slammed the door and went around to the driver's side. So much for pleasantries.

When they were locked safely inside the car again, Alec removed the keys from the ignition and threw them under his seat.

"Now that we're not risking our lives in rush-hour traffic, why don't you cut the BS and level with me for a change?" He leaned an elbow on the leather armrest between their seats, crowding her even with the console between them. "What is it that's getting you tied up in knots all of a sudden? And don't try to give me some crap about the near miss at my apartment. We couldn't have handled that any better."

She resisted the urge to swipe a hand across her forehead or maybe massage her temples. Instead she concentrated on a messenger streaking past the car on a bicycle, his legs pumping as though his life depended on whatever he carried in his satchel. Why hadn't she chosen a job with those kinds of clear-cut goals? Deliver the package. Simple. Focused.

She felt herself calming down a little bit. Until Alec's voice slid into her faraway thoughts.

"I don't give a rat's ass when we get to the Raven Club, by the way." He reached beneath the seat to adjust the position back several inches. "I'm in no hurry to find out anything about the damn carjacking when all I really want to know is what's messing with your head, Vanessa."

He wasn't going to take them to the Raven Club? Of all the obnoxious ways he could choose to piss her off and interfere with her job...

She might have railed at him, but before she could spit back a retort, her brain simmered down enough to acknowledge he hadn't said he *wasn't* taking her, just that he didn't care when they went. She was damn well losing her mind from stress and worry and the strange mental collision of her past and present last night.

Ever since she'd been hauled from Alec's car, she'd told herself that it would not be an act that went unpunished.

Unprosecuted, rather.

She'd find out who'd tried to scare the living daylights out of her last night, and she'd put them on trial for the crime. It would be one small victory to take the place of the bigger battle she hadn't won. Could never win now.

One way or another, she meant to put her old ghosts to rest.

10

"YOU MAY NOT CARE when we get to this hole-in-the-wall bar, but I do." Vanessa drummed her fingers on the leather armrest, her impatience tapping his conscience but only until he remembered how much she needed to settle down. Regroup.

Shrugging, he tipped back in the driver's seat a little more and peeled off his exterminator suit.

"Sorry. I need answers and I'm not of a mind to move until I get them."

Her silence was deliberate, pointed, but blessedly brief. After her moments of utter quiet, she started tugging off her bug-blaster outfit, too.

"Look, I've never shared jack about my past with anyone because I don't think it's anybody's business, but in the interest of a smooth partnership today, I'm going to make an exception for you." She threw the protective gear in her back seat on top of his and shifted in her seat to face him.

He waited. Hoped he hadn't made a mistake in pushing her.

"I grew up in the South Bronx. It's a little piece of

me I'll never fully escape." She dragged in a long breath. "But my sister was shot in a drive-by on 172nd Street just before I graduated college and I've never forgiven the local police, or my long-ago neighbors, for basically doing nothing about it."

She held her head high, her gaze clear and focused, but Alec couldn't mistake the pain in her voice. The regret. Anger.

He curled his fingers around hers, at a loss how to comfort a woman who seemed utterly self-sufficient. Defensive.

"I'm so damn sorry, Vanessa." The words seemed like precious little to offer a woman who'd obviously confronted her share of hardship. They were all he had at the moment, however.

"She's okay." Vanessa turned her gaze out the windshield, staring out over the waterfront now that one of the delivery trucks pulled out of view in a wake of diesel smoke. "It took a long time to recover the use of her leg, but she fought her way through therapy and she managed pretty well with a cane. She's so strong—so stubborn—she wouldn't let anyone help her through the rough times."

"Did they ever catch who did it?" He asked even though he suspected the answer. Instinct told him Vanessa harbored plenty of anger about the incident.

"No." Her brows slashed downward in a forbidding frown as she stared out the window. "The only person who came forward with evidence changed his testimony after a local gang got ahold of him. And apparently anybody else who might have seen anything that day knew better than to speak up. Drive-bys used to be a way of life back then, but if I hadn't been preoccupied…"

"Don't tell me you blame yourself." As a cop, she should know better than most people how random that kind of violence could be. "Nobody can be prepared for something like that."

"You don't understand. I wasn't just unprepared. I was *oblivious*. It was the end of the school year and I was caught up in some new guy I was dating and excited to tell my sister about a new internship available with a high-profile financial adviser…" She trailed off, her voice as far away as her eyes. "Having grown up in that kind of neighborhood, I knew better than to let my guard slip. And I sure as hell know better than to toss my guard to the four winds to indulge my own wants."

"But she's okay now." He needed to repeat it to remind himself of the fact. To remind Vanessa. "Does she still hold it against you?"

"Gena has never blamed me for a second."

A good thing. Alec would have had to pay her a visit if she did. Vanessa obviously carried around enough guilt for both of them.

"You said your sister is an attorney now. Is she a fearless crime fighter, too?" He wondered if this sibling was as kick-butt cool as Vanessa. Still, he hated to think Vanessa had honed all that strength of hers because she'd watched her sister fall from a gangster's bullet.

No wonder the carjacking had thrown her for such a loop. It must have been like reliving a nightmare for her.

"She's actually a public defender." A wry smile spread over her lips, reminding him how long it had been since he'd tasted her. Touched her.

"Can you imagine? I changed my whole focus in life so I could go after the creeps who shot her down and she takes a position protecting the rights of the city's worst offenders. Go figure."

Alec let the words sink in, needing an extra minute to process what he thought he heard as late-afternoon gridlock a few streets over erupted into a steady blast of blowing horns. "You mean you didn't always want to be a cop?"

"I was almost done with my MBA when Gena…I got the degree even though I didn't attend the last couple weeks of classes, but my whole life view changed once I started spending every day holding her hand in the intensive care unit." She rolled her eyes. "It's hard to give a rip about some fat corporate bottom line when your sister's struggling for her life."

"You wanted to go into high finance? Consulting?" He got a quick mental image of Vanessa in a power suit with a short skirt. Very un-PC but still sexy as hell.

"Does it matter?" Shaking her head, she traced the H-shaped pattern on the stick shift. "I was young and naive and I wanted to take on the world with a few good grades and a lot of ambition, but you don't see me tooling around the world in a private jet while I conduct business with the Japanese markets, do you?"

"I see you succeeding." Hell, didn't she get that same visual in her head? She could knock him on his ass with a sweep of her strong legs or even a breathy sigh, and he didn't fall for many women. For that matter, he didn't hit the mat in his self-defense class for anyone, yet she'd taken him down by surprising him. "Do you ever wish you were on the corporate jet?"

If his life were different now, if he hadn't spent the past six months in hiding, he'd whisk her away fast enough to have her sipping champagne before supper. The thought made him more determined than ever to pull the carpet out from under the greedy bastards he called partners.

"No," she answered a little too quickly as she straightened in her seat. "I've found my purpose."

"It's more than a lot of people have." His uncle came to mind. What was Sergio's purpose? To break knee-caps so he could drive a Cadillac? "What you do is noble. Important."

"Thank you." She tightened the band around her braid, her gaze skittering back to the view outside the car where seagulls fought over the heaping refuse in a trash can outside a nearby fish market.

"But that doesn't count for a whole hell of a lot if you're not happy."

"Who says I'm not happy?"

"You don't have to be a detective to figure that one out." What did she take him for? He had eyes. He could see she wasn't exactly falling all over herself with spontaneous joy.

"Look. You wanted to know what the deal was with me and my reticence to cavort around the Bronx. Now you know."

"And you think I'm satisfied? Hell, Vanessa, I wanted to know so I could help you, not because of some stupid intellectual curiosity." He reached for her, skimmed a hand down her cheek since his every other attempt to connect with her seemed to have failed. But this—the physical thing between them—it kicked in right on cue, igniting a flame that neither of them could ignore. He could see her response in her eyes, feel the subtle change in the rhythm of her breath.

"You can't help me."

"Only if you don't let me." His fingers slid down the length of her neck, dipping into the collar of her shirt to touch the smooth skin of her shoulder. The satin of one slender bra strap.

"The shooting happened a long time ago. My sister is over it. I don't know why I can't seem to lay the whole thing to rest." She wrapped her fingers around his wrist.

To hold him there? Or to make sure his touch didn't stray any lower?

Not that he had any intention of undressing her here, on the outskirts of East Harlem in her car, for crying out loud.

"I'm don't mean to minimize what your sister went through, but she had the grueling demands of physical therapy to work through. A tangible way to sweat out her anger and pain. And on the other side of her effort was healing. Recovery." He saw her shaking her head, already rejecting his words. He plowed on anyway, determined to give her something. At least prove he was listening and not looking for ways to peel off her clothes. "You didn't have that. You got to see her whole ordeal up close and personal, with no outlet for the pain, no healing for the guilt."

She didn't say anything for a long moment, her expression frozen somehow until she blinked fast. Made a little yelping noise deep with her throat.

Ah, damn.

He'd wanted to help her. Connect with her. But he didn't think he could forgive himself if he'd made this strong, independent woman cry.

Reaching across the console, he opened his arms to her, knowing their trip to the Raven Club would have to wait. Vanessa had become more important to him than any half-baked vengeance plot he might have in mind for whoever was trying to frame him. Right now, nothing seemed more important to him than holding her.

VANESSA KNEW IF SHE ACCEPTED the full benefit of Alec's touch, she'd lose whatever tenuous grip on her emotions she still maintained. Burying her head against his shoulder, feeling his arms wrap around her would somehow force her to connect with long-suppressed emotions about the shooting, the same way their bedroom encounter had ripped away all the old fears and hang-ups she'd come to associate with sex.

The prospect scared her as much as any trip to the Bronx. Possibly more, since she couldn't use a gun for protection in the slippery world of emotions.

She settled for leaning halfway into his embrace, resting her head on the comforting strength of his bicep, instead of hurling herself into his arms. If Alec thought her hesitance was odd, he didn't say anything about it. He kissed the top of her head and curled his arm around her shoulders to stray down her arm and rub her back.

He held her that way until she found her voice. Swallowed back tears she resented. Damn it, but she needed to pull herself together. She'd give herself another minute here, a few more moments to accept his comfort and then she'd find the strength to put this behind her again.

"Gena told me once she doesn't even remember what happened that day. The shots. The tire squeals. The shouting. None of it." She'd envied her sister the forgetting, and then felt guilty for envying a woman who'd been through more pain than Vanessa could fathom. "I remember every minute detail, every gulping breath my sister took after the bullet penetrated her skin, every retreating footstep as all the people around us ran for cover and left us there alone with some dumb-ass talk-radio station blaring from a window nearby. But despite all the damn clarity, I could never remember the single most important piece of information the cops wanted to know."

"No license plate." He muttered the words into her hair, the scent of his aftershave attracting her for a deeper sniff.

"No license plate. I had a vague sense of a big, black SUV roaring away but I couldn't ID the make and model." She'd beat herself up about it for weeks. Months. Hypnosis hadn't helped, either, since the hypnotist swore she simply hadn't been watching the vehicle. Vanessa's eyes had been focused on her sister. "I told myself that I would never make that mistake again as a cop, and I signed on for the NYPD a few weeks after the shooting."

The first couple of months on the job had been a blur, but she'd pulled herself out of it quickly enough in deference to her sister and the hardships she'd endured in ICU and later during rehabilitation.

"You never looked back on your abrupt career change?" His hand paused in its gentle massage of her shoulders. "Do you foresee a time when you'll say that you've atoned for those ten seconds when you looked down at your sister instead of at a speeding car?"

Sitting up straight, she realized she'd indulged in the comfort of Alec's touch for too long if he was asking her questions like that. Still, she couldn't deny she would have sat there forever as long as his hands remained on her. Stroking.

"It's not a matter of atoning for anything. As a detective, I'm right where I need to be to make a difference and that's a hell of a lot more important to me these days than how much money I can make."

"No regrets about bypassing the business world after putting in all those hours for a degree?"

"I think it makes more sense to look forward than to stare back at the past, don't you?" She shifted in her seat, focusing her attention back to the street and all the things they needed to accomplish today.

Rehashing old wounds wouldn't solve anything, especially not with Alec looking on, witnessing her weaknesses. She had enough trouble forgiving herself for the past. Why share her failings with a man who already knew way too much about her?

"I think it's tough to move forward when the past has you in a choke hold, but that's just me."

She felt his gaze from the other side of the car, his scrutiny not letting her slough off the conversation as quickly as she would have preferred. Damn it.

"Choke hold or not, we'd better get to the Raven Club before it gets any later. Once the bar starts filling up, no one is going to talk to us."

"I'm not dragging you through the most lawless beer joint on the south side just so we can find out who jumped us last night." He shook his head, making no move to start the car. "I had no business asking you to skirt the rules and help me figure out who's trying to frame me in the first place."

"You can't back out now just because I've made a few mistakes in the past." She never would have told him a damn thing about herself if she'd known he'd try to pull some macho protector crap. "I can take care of myself, Alec, and I'm going to the Raven whether you want to join me or not."

"You know how many drive-bys have happened on that very block, Vanessa?" He leaned into her space, his voice lowered.

"Not a clue. But I know if I can put away those guys who jumped us last night, maybe I can prevent a few more." Even if it scared her to set foot in there. Only an idiot wouldn't feel a few qualms about entering such a notoriously dangerous place.

"Shit." Alec reached forward to start the car although he clearly wasn't happy about it. "We go in there, get our answers and go home. *Together.*"

"I've got my car and we're almost positive no one's following us now that your uncle is in jail." To spend more time with Alec meant falling into bed. The sexual attraction was so thick, so elemental, she'd be naive to think they could be around each other alone for ten minutes and not wind up touching. "I can go back to my place tonight. We can figure out how to keep you safe from your partners tomorrow."

"You haven't even looked at the disks we risked our necks to retrieve."

"Then make me some copies, and I'll look at them

tonight." When she was alone. When her brain engaged again after a day of relentless sex thoughts.

"For now, you trust me." He seemed satisfied at the thought as he put the car in reverse. "That's a good thing. But about us parting company tonight? Not gonna happen."

VANESSA'S ANGER didn't linger.

Alec sort of wished it had as they sped over the Third Street Bridge into the South Bronx. Instead, her frustrations morphed into a cold wariness he suspected stemmed from old ghosts about the area where she'd grown up. And although her watchfulness didn't look much like fear, Alec saw past her careful facade better now. He could almost hear her counting the seconds it would take her to go for her gun if the need arose.

Yeah, he'd rather have had her pissed off at him any day.

A few minutes later he pulled into a parking space on the street, situating the vehicle near the small lot that served the bar. Only a few cars filled the spaces now, since the sun hadn't set yet. But in another hour, the club would be crawling with every stripe of punk imaginable out for a good time on a Friday night.

"Maybe we shouldn't go in together." Vanessa blurted out a thought that—surprisingly—mirrored his own.

He wanted to find out who'd taken his car last night, but not at the expense of Vanessa's safety.

"How about I go in and ask the questions on my own? If I'm not out in ten minutes, you can call for every cop in the city to haul me in. Deal?"

"I just meant we might look too much like law enforcement if we go in there together."

"So I'll go in alone." He didn't care what her reasons were for not going in together—he'd jump on any opportunity to keep her safe in the car.

"Unless we went in there like a couple." Her eyes slid over his chest. Lower. Then back up to his face. "Sort of all over each other. Then we wouldn't look like cops."

"Appealing as it sounds to be all over you—an assignment I could fulfill with ease, by the way—I think we'd still raise a flag just because of our clothes. We look too out of place to hang out here."

"Not enough bling?" Her smile didn't begin to ease the worries gnawing at his gut from picturing her in a hangout like this.

"Either that, or we need to go the other way and look a little more street smart. People around here are either struggling to make a living or their pockets are overflowing with money skimmed off everyone else." He scruffed up his hair just enough to blend in, then untucked his shirt.

He watched Vanessa start to do the same when a car driving into the Raven Club parking lot caught his eye out the window.

A way-too-freaking-familiar car.

"Wait." He grabbed Vanessa's hand to halt her flurry

of movement in the seat beside him. "One of my partners just drove into the lot."

Sinking deeper into his seat, he dragged Vanessa with him.

"McPherson?" she whispered as she watched, even though there wasn't much of a chance anyone would overhear them inside the car.

"No. Vercelli. You never spoke to them?" He hit the button to lower the power window on her side of the car, opening it just a crack.

She shook her head, eyes still trained on his business associate who fell firmly into the "bling" category as he stepped out of his Lexus and walked toward a side entrance to the Raven Club. "My assignment to find you came from higher up."

Tension threaded through him as they watched his partner—a guy he'd gone to college with, a guy who'd been a frat brother, a guy he'd trusted. Mark didn't make it to the back entrance before the door swung open, revealing a tall kid in a wrinkled tuxedo shirt and crooked tie.

Mark's nephew.

Recognition pummeled Alec, hitting him from all sides at once as he put the pieces together. The vaguely familiar eyes of the carjacker last night. The presence of his partner in the Bronx when Alec had never known Mark to set foot out of Brooklyn.

He didn't realize he'd started swearing under his breath until Vanessa jabbed him in the leg.

"Shh." She cocked her head at a strange angle to put her ear closer to the crack in the window.

Too bad Alec had all the evidence necessary. Then again, he didn't need to make a case against the guy who was supposed to be his friend.

He only needed to get even.

Fury flooded his veins as he remembered the brute force the carjackers had used on Vanessa. The way her soft skin has been torn away from her spine when they'd dragged her across the street.

They were in as much danger—and more—than even he'd realized.

Starting the car, he didn't much care if Mark saw them leave. The important thing was to get Vanessa out of here before Alec lost it and took out his alleged good friend right here on Tremont Street for all the world to see.

"What are you doing?" Vanessa turned her face to the side, mouthing the words at Alec as he squealed out of the parking space and into a U-turn on the street. "We didn't even get to question anyone at the bar."

"I take it you don't recognize the punk in the bow tie?"

Hitting the gas, he swerved around a parked truck and ran a light just as it turned red.

"The kid who looked like a waiter?"

"That kid waved a 9 mm in your face last night, Vanessa. I hope your partner is still on duty because you can tell him you just found your carjacker."

11

HER HEART LODGED in her throat, as much from the U-turn as Alec's positive ID of the rumpled waiter.

"You're kidding." She craned her neck to stare out the back window, knowing Alec wouldn't joke about something that had scared her to the roots of her hair. Roots that were going to be gray in no time if she kept hanging out with Alec.

"Definitely not kidding." He slid onto the entrance ramp for the Bruckner Expressway without too much hassle now that dusk was falling and traffic had thinned out. "Vercelli must have hired the kid to follow you after he made the bogus complaint to the NYPD about me embezzling funds."

"And I led him right to you." For the first time, she regretted doing such a good job on the force. What might this guy have done to Alec if he'd been alone last night on that dark alley in the Bronx?

She shuddered with the thought.

"Lucky for me, you're going to be able to back up my story with the police department." He seemed content to let her off the hook, his tense muscles relaxing the more distance they put between them and the Raven Club. "You've seen enough now to know that at least one of my partners wants me dead, scared or in jail. You can make arrests. Convict the bastards."

"With what? My say-so?" After seeing the way her sister's case had dried up into nothing, Vanessa wouldn't risk letting Alec's enemies walk away. "We don't have physical evidence yet. We need to find your car. Scare up a paper trail."

"You've got the disks." He jerked a thumb toward the back seat where he'd stored the package they'd taken from above his ceiling tiles.

"Which may or may not have survived the temperature fluctuations of being stored near the ductwork. And beyond that, we know how easy it can be to tamper with that kind of data. Convicting your partners of anything is going to require more time. More legwork."

"Fine. But let the police do it. I'm ready to go into the cop shop with you now that my uncle's behind bars and you've seen my partners' got it in for me." Downshifting for a patch of gridlock around a construction site along the shoulder of the expressway, Alec glanced over at her. "They won't try to arrest me if we have reason to question the evidence offered up by my partners, right?"

"Right. In theory."

"What the hell is that supposed to mean?" He checked his rearview mirror, probably watching to see if they'd been followed. The way she should be doing.

Her objectivity and professional distance seemed to be slipping away from her by the hour, distorted by the presence of emotions she'd never felt before, twisted even further by her unease at being in this part of town.

Thankfully, they'd be leaving the Bronx behind soon. The exit for a bridge back to Manhattan was just a couple of miles ahead.

"I'm a little worried about why my lieutenant sent me out after you in the first place without asking me to look into McPherson Real Estate and the legitimacy of your partners' complaint. I'd just assumed he'd done the homework and thought we needed to bring you in. But since he didn't bother and still had me come after you…"

"You think there's corruption in your department?"

"I don't know, but I don't want to guarantee they'll let you go without having more evidence to back up your claim." She didn't think the head of their precinct would be involved in anything illegal. No way. No how.

But she couldn't deny a small niggle of worry about Lieutenant Durant looking out for some of his own investments if he'd allowed McPherson to press their claim without checking into the details behind it.

"Well I'm not going back into hiding." He sped past the exit that would take them to Manhattan and continued south toward Queens. "I'm buying back my freedom one way or another, and if the cops won't help me reclaim my life then I'll have to take matters into my own hands."

"What do you mean?" She couldn't help but visualize the gun she knew was secured at his waist. How far would he go to recover his old life?

"I mean I'm going to call on my personal resources to get the evidence we need and put these guys behind bars."

"And you're going to find evidence in Queens?" She squinted up at the signs overhead, wondering what on earth he had in mind.

"LaGuardia. I've got a private plane out there and I can have a pilot meet us at the airport within half an hour." He peered over at her from the driver's side, his dark eyes intense. "Welcome to the world of high finance, Vanessa. You're about to get a bird's-eye view of the world you walked away from when you turned your back on the MBA."

He had a jet.

The information didn't fully penetrate Vanessa's brain until she took in the lines of the Cessna in a section of LaGuardia Airport she'd never seen up close and personal. There was no check-in process. No mile-long line at a ticket counter. Alec simply shook hands with the pilot, who apparently appeared on call from some sort of air-management company, and before she knew it, the stairs to the plane were being unfurled from the cabin door.

"Ready?" Alec nodded toward the aircraft, the bright halogen lamps ringing the boarding area casting the whole bizarre world of a corporate magnate in a surreal light. She'd had dreams that looked sort of like this. Only there hadn't been a guy with a gun carting her aboard the plane.

"Ready for what?" The stresses of the last twenty-four hours had taken a toll on her clear thinking, clouding her brain with an assortment of worries mixed up with her past. "I have no idea where you're going and for all I know, you could be trying to flee the country. I'd be ten kinds of an idiot to get on that plane with you when I'm just supposed to be locating you and bringing you into the station for some questions."

"And why would I head to the border *now* after I've been hiding under my uncle's nose in the Bronx for six months while he was still a free man?" He slipped his hand beneath her hair and massaged the back of her neck with soft, subtle pressure. "I've got a place in the Hamptons, close to where Sergio keeps his mistress. We can ask Donata some questions, find out where they're keeping my uncle and figure out if he's been scheming with my partners or not."

She rested her palm on the metal handrail to the stairs leading up to the plane, wading through too many thoughts to name. The idea of meeting a woman who had the hots for Alec held zero appeal. Of course, the idea of him going to speak with Kittykat alone sort of sucked, too.

"And you want me to go with you, even though Sergio is in jail? I could go back to the precinct now. Find out more about what the police have on your uncle. Possibly we could talk to him while he's safely behind bars."

"The threat to you is stronger than ever since my partner knows we've joined forces." He gripped both her shoulders, steadying her while he broadcast the reality she didn't want to see. "He obviously wants me out of the business, and my share is worth a hell of a lot of money. He's in too deep to let us walk away now."

Vanessa felt herself relenting, knowing she had no choice but to see this thing through with Alec. She didn't understand how her life had gotten tangled up with his so fast, but she also knew she wouldn't walk away until he was safe from the web of deceit woven around him by people he should have been able to trust. Like his partners, she was in too deep now. Committed to a cause.

Because surely it was the cause and not just the man himself that had her wearing disguises, calling in sick to work and now—good God—jumping on a plane to the Hamptons.

"Any idea why this guy you've worked with for years would turn on you?" That part bothered her, contradicted her understanding of human nature—limited though it might be.

As much as she resented the violence in the part of town where she'd grown up, at least you knew who the enemy was. Gangsters advertised their allegiances in the colors they wore, the tattoos they branded on their bodies. But in Alec's world, the enemy remained more subtle, showing up in your own family or among your friends.

Alec peered out over the tarmac where a few other private jets waited. Squinting against the halogen lights, he turned toward the parking area where cars dropped off the privileged few who could take advantage of this kind of luxury.

"Could we discuss this once we are airborne?" He lowered his voice even though the pilot had disappeared inside the plane. "I'm paying this guy by the hour and I'll be glad to put some distance between us and Vercelli. He won't know where we've gone until we land, and even then it will take him a while to catch up."

But would she be safer to take off for parts unknown with a mysterious man who carried a gun and cursed in multiple languages? Add in his major sex appeal and the fact that one night with him had dredged up emotions she didn't even know she possessed, and Alec Messina was a very dangerous man.

That didn't stop her from climbing the stairs to the Cessna, though. One way or another, she would help Alec gather whatever evidence necessary to see justice served.

But as Alec pulled up the stairway and locked the door, effectively sealing them inside the passenger compartment all alone, she didn't have any illusion that she would be safe.

ALEC STARED AT VANESSA still standing in the aisle of the eight-passenger plane and told himself this was a really bad time to think about sex.

In the past twenty-four hours, she'd been held at gunpoint, abandoned in the middle of urban hell by carjackers and dragged semi-unwillingly into Alec's world of deception and danger. She was perfectly within her rights not to be in the mood for sex. But then again, they'd already lit one another's sexual fires twice in the short time they'd known one another.

Which was probably why he found himself thinking about taking her clothes off now that they were alone again in the safety of his plane. The pilot's cabin was sealed shut during flight for both parties' protection. The flight to the Hamptons would be short—less than an hour counting the wait for takeoff—but still offered plenty of time to touch her the way he'd wanted to all day. Ever since they'd gotten dressed this morning, actually.

"Nice ride you've got here." She smoothed her hand over one of the seats he'd had reupholstered when he'd bought the plane two years ago. The scent of the leather lingered even after the new carpet smell had faded the first year.

"Thanks." He didn't want to talk about the plane. He wanted to give her a better ride. One she wouldn't forget after their flight was over. But out of deference to her, he reined in his thoughts. Okay, maybe not his thoughts, but he sure as hell kept better control of his mouth. "I got sick of trying to arrange charter flights as often as I needed them. I told myself this would save me money in the long run, but it was also sort of self-ish. Always wanted a plane."

He ran a palm over the polished walnut cabinet housing the media center at the front of the passenger cabin. The plane had been a cool toy, but it hadn't come close to filling the gaps in life. It hadn't been until more recently that he'd keyed into the need to give something back after all the ways he'd cashed in with his business. Teaching self-defense to smart-ass kids like Easy had actually bought him more true satisfaction than the expensive toy.

A welcome wake-up call.

"And since you must realize that showing up at your house in the Hamptons via plane is going to quickly announce your presence around the neighborhood, I can only assume you want to make your arrival known?"

He gestured to the chair she'd been standing behind. Maybe he'd stop thinking about peeling the clothes from her body if he were seated beside her instead of standing across from her and appreciating each and every nuance of her curves. It could happen.

Not.

"I'm done with hiding, thanks to you." Her arrival at the rec center last night had spurred him out of the routine he'd fallen into. Made him realize he had more to accomplish. "And if there's anyone in all of Long Island who hasn't heard I'm back, they'll know the truth soon after we pay a visit to Donata. She's very good about spreading the latest news."

Vanessa slid into the seat, her long, lean body pressing into the sleek expanse of leather. "I might have to skip the visit to any woman who signs herself as 'Your Pussy.' Call me old-fashioned, but I'm not much into sharing a man I'm sleeping with, even if the sex came about under extenuating circumstances."

"And just what's that supposed to mean?" He pushed an intercom button behind the media center and informed the pilot they were ready to take off. Then, switching off the system, he sat down in the seat next to Vanessa.

He'd been prepared to sit across the aisle from her to give her some breathing room, but he'd be damned if he would deny himself the pleasure of her proximity if she was going to play head games with him. "Are you trying to suggest that sex between us wasn't inevitable? That you could have somehow avoided getting involved with me if we hadn't been thrown into the carjacking situation?"

She turned to glare at him, her dark, smoky stare turning him on even though she happened to look damn annoyed with him right about now.

"I beg your pardon?" She crossed her arms, adopting a classic battle pose. "*Inevitable?* Don't you think that might be overstating the case just a little?"

"Hell no. And buckle up, damn it." He jammed his own seat belt into place, knowing there were a hundred other things they should be discussing before he walked back into his world after a six-month absence, but right now, this seemed more important. "I don't care how traumatic things were last night. We felt the heat of this attraction long before we slid into the Mercedes."

She shook her head, her long, dark hair dancing with the movement. "Feeling an attraction isn't the same as acting on it. I think I could have scavenged a whole lot more self-control without the memory of a gun jammed into my temple."

Damn. He was being insensitive and he knew it. Last night *had* been rough. He just didn't like to think she'd been driven to his bed for any reason other than that she wanted him. Badly.

"You're right." He didn't have any desire to argue with her now that they could let their guards down for the first time since they'd left his apartment that morning. Reaching across the armrest that separated them, he stroked a gentle touch along her shoulder. "I just wish I didn't have to thank a couple of street punks for bringing you to me because I wanted you from the second you volunteered to demonstrate a self-defense move for me."

A hint of a smile played over her full lips as the plane inched forward, the sound of the engines gently rumbling through the cabin no matter how much noise-deadening insulation he'd installed beneath the carpet.

"You looked like you were in need of a worthy opponent."

"Except I don't want to keep being your adversary." Learning about her sister's accident made him understand why her first instinct was to shove people away. She didn't trust the legal system, and Alec suspected half her reason for going into law enforcement had been to do a better job than the cops had done on her sister's behalf.

But he wouldn't be another guy she mistrusted, another man she suspected wouldn't hold up his end of the bargain. He just wasn't sure what she expected from him.

"Which brings to mind an interesting point." She kept her posture ramrod straight, no hint of relaxing into his touch. "If we're not adversaries anymore, what are we? Where do you see this thing going once we can nail your partner?"

He hadn't expected that kind of candidness from her. Not here. Not yet. The question felt like an opportunity, a chance to reach for something better than he'd ever had before.

But he must have taken too long to answer since she exhaled an exasperated, "Never mind."

"No. I'm just thinking." He wouldn't let her yank the question back now. "I haven't really thought about the future in so long. I've been buried in work with the center, just keeping my head above water."

"Must be hell when you don't have access to your private jet." She crossed one gorgeous leg over the other, making it difficult to think about any future beyond undressing her.

"You're just pissed because you know you would have been flying around in your own Cessna by now if you had followed your dreams after college." He slipped his hand inside the cuff of her jacket sleeve, grateful for any access to her body.

Beneath them, the hum of the engines grew louder as the plane picked up speed. They must have received the go-ahead to take off because the aircraft launched forward fast enough to gently pin them in their seats.

"I know no such thing." She closed her eyes for a moment as they lifted into the air, her lashes grazing her cheek in a rare display of relaxation—enjoyment?—for a woman who seemed to have been born wary. "There are thousands of MBAs in this city and only a tiny percentage of them achieve the kind of success you have."

"One of the things Vercelli told me once was that people do business with us because they want to foster goodwill with the mob." He didn't appreciate the reminder that all of his success might not be built on hard work alone. "How messed up is that? But I never did a freaking thing to suggest to anyone I ever worked with that I had a connection to Sergio."

"I didn't mean to say your business is flourishing because of that." A crease furrowed the smooth surface of her forehead. "I just meant to point out that no degree guarantees any kind of success. And I can promise you that no matter how close your ties to organized crime, you wouldn't have this kind of success in real estate without a canny eye for development and a shrewd knowledge of what properties to buy. Business sense isn't granted to any man because he carries a gun, and I've arrested enough nimrods with weapons to know this for an absolute fact."

The plane leveled off as they reached their cruising altitude, the engine noise fading into the background, or perhaps Alec just grew more accustomed to the muted rumble.

"Thanks." Her frank assessment pleased him more than a garden-variety compliment tossed out by women in his past. Donata's interest in him had coincided precisely with the moment she found out he had as much net worth as his uncle, and his business was legal to boot. He'd been happy to help Donata get out from under Sergio's thumb until he realized she'd never leave his protection without another man lined up to bankroll her expensive habits. "And for the record, I know you'd excel at anything you wanted to do. The MBA is a piece of paper. It's *you* I have faith in."

"Really?" She kept her tone skeptical, but Alec didn't miss the hint of pleasure in her voice. "You may have missed your calling as a motivational speaker."

He skimmed a touch along the inside of her elbow, his knuckles grazing the fabric of her linen jacket as he adjusted his hand for a better angle.

"I happen to be feeling pretty damn motivated right now." He hadn't meant to say it; the words just propelled themselves from his mouth.

But sitting next to her here in their bubble of privacy

soaring over Long Island, he found it difficult to remember why he should keep his hands to himself. Her dark hair glowed with subtle bronze highlights under the lone reading lamp they'd left on above their seats. The supple leather creaked quietly behind her shoulders as she pressed herself deeper into the seat.

"Motivated for what? Seducing a city detective into your personal mile-high club?" Her words were softly chiding, but her breath quickened, her chest expanding and falling a little faster than before.

Not that his eyes were glued to her very admirable breasts, damn it.

"I can count on one hand the number of times I've had occasion to share this plane with clients and not once have I seduced any of them. I may have persuaded them to sign on the dotted line for a land deal or two, but I never cinched a mile-high quickie for myself." His fingers strayed up her arm, stretching the fabric of her jacket as far as it would go to accommodate his touch. He could feel her heart pounding at the contact, knew she experienced the same relentless tug of attraction that had never been far from his mind today.

"There's where you've been getting it all wrong, Messina." She tipped her head back against the seat, a silent gesture of surrender if ever he'd seen one. "You can't think in terms of a quickie when you're flying around in a private jet. Look at this place. A woman is bound to be more in the mood for the five-star treatment once she sets foot in here."

His hand stilled on her arm. Lust blindsided him, seriously impairing his ability to form sentences.

"I seem to have lost my capacity for thought somewhere between 'five' and 'star.' Can you clarify for me that you're not going to be offended if I rip those clothes off you right now?"

"The way I see it, your uncle's mistress is going to spit nails if she figures out we're sleeping together, so I'd prefer to go into this meeting with a clear memory of why I took the risk."

"Was that a yes?" His blood slammed through his veins with such force he couldn't be entirely sure.

"Damn it, Alec, I'm going to be seriously offended if you *don't* rip these clothes off me now."

12

A WOMAN COULDN'T MAKE HERSELF more clear than that.

Vanessa held her breath as she waited for Alec to comprehend her meaning. She had dealt with enough reality in the past five years to recognize she needed an escape today—if only for a few stolen moments. Alec made a better fantasy man than she could have ever dreamed up on her own. Sure, he might have a few wicked ways about him. And she understood that he possessed a dark, earthy quality some women might not appreciate.

But Vanessa wasn't most women.

She could admire a man who didn't take his jet to some remote Caribbean island the moment times got tough in his real-estate business. With as much money as Alec must have access to, he could have gone into hiding anywhere around the globe, yet he'd opted to hang out in the Bronx where he'd taught kids how to survive. How to fight back.

Maybe Alec needed this escape right now as badly as she did.

"Come here." His command was soft but unmistakable as he lifted the armrest between them and unbuckled her seat belt. His fingers maneuvered the metal buckle, brushing along her hip for a fraction of a second. Long enough to send a sensual flutter along her nerves.

Uncertainty—a foreign sensation—held her motionless. She'd expected him to take her at her word about ripping her clothes off. Their encounter the night before, and even that morning had been marked by deep hunger and restless need, driven by an elemental urge to connect.

She hadn't anticipated this slow watchfulness on his part now, his eyes brimming with heat he seemed to be keeping carefully controlled.

"Over there?" She settled for walking her fingers up his lower thigh.

"Yeah." He trapped her fingers and dragged her closer, tugging her toward his lap. "Over here. Where I can get a better look at you."

She found herself leaning, reaching, stretching out across his chest as he wrapped his arms around her until she half sprawled over his lap, her legs the only part of her body that lingered in her vacated seat.

She didn't need to hold on to him since he held her right where he wanted her. Still, she found her hands seeking his shoulders, her fingers gliding along his shirt to the corded strength of his neck.

"Is this close enough for you?" Her breasts tightened

at his proximity, the anticipation of his touch making every inch of her skin hot with awareness.

"Not nearly enough, and I think you know that." He tightened his hold on her with one arm while letting go with the other. Reaching up to the reading light, he clicked off the small lamp, casting the passenger cabin in darkness except for a softly illuminated red Exit sign above the door.

While the dark soothed her, easing any leftover doubts about the wisdom of being with him again, she couldn't help but remember that he'd brought her closer in order to look at her.

Or so he said.

"You'll never see me now." She palmed his cheek, her fingers sifting into the dark hair along his temple. The motion brought her breasts that much closer to his chest, the ache for him growing sharper every second she was suspended over his lap.

"I don't think you're ready to let me see you the way I want to yet." He reached into the V of her shirt, using the tips of three fingers to stroke down the center of her chest. "I want to know all about you. See the parts of you bared that you've never shown to anyone else."

His soft caress distracted her, robbing her focus as the feel of lace over her nipples suddenly constrained her unbearably, the fabric agitating her until she longed to do the clothes ripping for him.

"I'm no innocent, Alec." As much as she wanted

him, she didn't want to deceive him on that score. "I've been seen a time or two before."

"No." He shook his head while he blew a warm stream of air from his lips to the patch of exposed skin just above the valley of her cleavage. "I don't think anybody else has ever touched you the way you let me touch you last night. And next time I take your clothes off I want to be naked with you for real. Do you understand what I mean?"

She shook her head, not understanding at all. Possibly a little afraid to understand. Maybe the high altitude was starting to get to her.

"I want the five-star sex as much the next guy. But I don't think you find that with just anyone." He covered her hand with his and slid it down to his lips. Planting a kiss inside her palm, he flicked his tongue over her skin before lowering her hand. "We had that last night because we connected on a deeper level. And while recreational sex is cool, too, it's not something I can retreat to after getting a taste of what the real deal can be like."

"Are you telling me—" Her thoughts seemed to run from her struggling brain, and no matter how much she concentrated, they only hovered further out of her mental grasp. He couldn't be talking about deep and meaningful emotions, right? And yet, what else could he mean? "Last night was super-charged because of the fear. The adrenaline letdown. The cloak-and-dagger antics of getting into your apartment. That's not reality."

"Fear?" He slipped his hand beneath her jacket to lay on her waist, his thumb and forefinger playing barely there caresses up and down her side. "Is that what you were feeling when I poured drops of warm oil over your skin? Or when I licked each drop off you? Were you scared when I sat you on top of the dresser and drove into you like I'd never get enough?"

Her mouth went dry at the memories, her lips so hot and parched she had no choice but to bathe them with a swipe of her tongue.

A swipe Alec followed with his gaze. "Yeah, that's what I thought."

The warm red light from the Exit sign imbued his skin with a demonic glow, his probing questions confusing her when all she wanted was to lose herself in him, under him.

She couldn't let him make this too complicated when her thoughts were being pulled in ten directions, her energies devoted to her quest for justice and her heart still grappling with the old hurts from Gena's accident that they'd unwittingly brought to the surface today.

What had happened to her escape from reality?

"You know, maybe you've had a lot of time and experience to devote to figuring out exactly what kind of sex you like best." Moving slowly, carefully, she found the first button on his shirt and slid the smooth, round disk through the hole. Followed by another. "But before last night, it had been a really, really long time for me."

When he didn't say anything, didn't move, she decided to clarify. Press her case.

"Years. Several years." Not to put too fine a point on it. But damn. She wouldn't let him think she was Ms. Recreational, either. Undeterred, she kept up her slow conquest of his buttons. "Now that I find myself in a position to engage in sex that I really want, I'll be damned if you're going to go and make it too complicated for me."

"Years?"

She finished the last of the buttons, exposing the smooth, taut skin of his chest and the hint of rock-hard abs any woman would love to get her hands on.

And speaking of rock-hard…

"You know, I'm reconsidering the merits of a good, old-fashioned quickie—"

His mouth found hers with sudden swiftness, erasing any doubts she might have had about how much he wanted her. She'd figure out how to handle his request for more of her later, when she wasn't in the throes of urgent need.

His kiss came with just the right pressure, his lips demanding her response. The sound of their breathing mingled in her ears with the hum of the plane's engines, the dull roar plunging them deeper into their own world, cocooning them in white noise. The sounds even drowned out her thoughts, releasing her from the last of her fears about joining with Alec.

She wanted this—wanted him—with a frenzy she couldn't deny and a hunger that had only multiplied since the night before. Having experienced a taste of him once, she'd somehow gotten hooked.

He pulled back from her as if he'd run out of breath, as if he needed to break the live-wire connection they seemed to share. "You think I'm even capable of a quickie with you?"

Assuming it to be a rhetorical question since the bulge in his pants made him look pretty damn capable in her eyes, Vanessa kept her mouth shut. Shaking his head, he flicked the jacket off her shoulders, skewing the fabric of her T-shirt to one side to expose her bra strap.

"I want to feast on you like there's no tomorrow." He nipped at her bare shoulder, teeth grazing her skin and raising goose bumps.

Shivers licked over her at the idea of Alec tasting her deeply. Repeatedly.

No doubt, she'd arrive in the Hamptons still feverish and quaking with the tremors of her orgasms. Probably not practical, even if it sounded…incredible.

"Maybe I'd better take charge then." Shoving to her knees, she straddled his lap. She yanked his shirt off his shoulders, leaving his arms caught up in the crisp cotton. "And don't worry, I won't ever tell anyone that you engaged in something so sordid as recreational sex. It'll be our little secret."

He watched her with moody eyes, his gaze fastened to her face even when she whipped the T-shirt over her head. But when she slid off her bra, she could see him shift ever so slightly in his seat.

"Don't blink now, Alec." Kneeling over him, she

bent to whisper against his ear, making sure the soft curve of her breast grazed his bristly cheek as she shifted positions. "I wouldn't want you to miss anything."

He lifted his chin then, perhaps to look up at her, or maybe just to drag the rough edge of his jaw over the achingly tender softness of her breast. Her nipple puckered even tighter. Warmth pooled between her thighs, her body ready for him long before he'd taken off her clothes. Just like the night before.

Only this time, instead of him taking his time to peel her out of her clothes, here she was stripping things off for him, offering herself up for sexual conquest.

"Pretty sure of yourself, aren't you?" Alec's voice held a dangerous edge, a warning note she didn't have any intention of heeding.

His tongue darted across the taut nipple, the action sending an answering contraction between her legs, the pleasure intense enough to almost be painful.

She couldn't imagine what might happen if he licked her now. There.

In a flash, he freed himself from the shirt around his elbows, shaking the cotton loose onto the floor as he stretched up to steady her.

"I'm sure I want this." It was the only thing that seemed certain in her life. Whatever Alec could give her here, now, she would be signing on.

His arm banded around her back, her hips. He didn't pull her down to his lap, but drew her hips into his chest so that her sex butted up against the center of his ribs. The heat of him penetrated her jeans, reminding her how hot this ride would be, how much she needed just to let go and enjoy.

Maybe with a little incentive, Alec would see how much fun recreational sex could be.

SHE WANTED SOMETHING Alec knew damn well he couldn't give her.

Recreation?

Hell, couldn't women buy vibrators for that? He wanted more than just a good time with her and he wanted her to know it, but he wasn't dumb enough to let this opportunity pass him by. Until she understood that he was serious about getting to know her, he would seduce her into knowing *him*.

Unfair?

The woman carried a gun 24-7. She'd had years of experience fending off guys. As far as Alec could figure, only a moron would give her a chance to start putting up boundaries and relegating sex to a playtime activity.

He cupped the curve of her ass in his palms, nudging her hips tighter to his chest. She felt so good. So hot. The sweet scent of her sex made him even harder when he was already taxing his zipper.

Unfastening her jeans, he breathed a damp kiss onto the front of her panties, inciting a roll of her hips to make any stripper proud. Not that he planned to share the thought. Vanessa's kick-ass exterior housed a vulnerability he hadn't expected, a softness he wanted to protect no matter who wore the damn badge.

The mewling sounds of pleasure she made in her throat had him forgetting all about his noble intentions for next time he got her naked. He couldn't ignore the hip roll. Couldn't deny her soft moans for the completion he knew how to provide best thanks to the full, uninhibited access to her body last night.

There were benefits of watching and learning.

Lifting her in his arms, he laid her out on the leather seats, allowing her knees to dangle over the edge as he dragged her jeans from her legs. Her hair had sprung loose from her braid, providing a silky dark blanket for her bare skin against the buff-colored leather. From restless thighs to rising and falling breasts, every inch of her flushed pink even though he hadn't taken her to full-fledged orgasm yet.

Stepping out of his trousers, he withdrew a condom from his wallet before tossing his pants aside, unconcerned that his bare butt was mooning all of Long Island. He stepped away from the windows, closing in on Vanessa, determined to imprint himself on her consciousness as thoroughly as she'd already impressed him.

She didn't stay put on the seats where he'd left her. She rose up again, impatient hands reaching for him, skimming over his naked thighs and abs until she stroked his cock.

He hadn't expected that, hadn't meant to let her slow him down in his quest to bring her off before they landed. But his johnson bobbed toward her of its own volition whenever she let him go, his head too overloaded with the sheer impact of Vanessa to tell her no.

"I can't touch you enough. And I've been dying to try out a new trick you taught me." She peered up at him, her soft cheek stroking, skimming the length of his straining erection until she turned to blow a stream of warm air over him.

The same way he'd done to her breasts earlier.

"You know too much." He gritted the words between clenched teeth, knowing he didn't dare let her try out any more new tricks tonight. A red-hot twinge of sensation knifed down his spine and squeezed him by the balls, reminding him he had no time left before he was going to lose it with her. Here. Now.

His window for finesse vanished, he lifted her, hauled her up his body until they faced each other. He wanted to kiss her, explore her mouth and neck and that incredible valley between her breasts, but he was on borrowed time after the way she'd touched him.

"Turn around." He growled out the words, hoping she understood that he walked a sharp edge of desire now. One false move and he was done for.

She spun away from him easily, her breath coming fast and shallow as she arched her back, bending at the waist just enough to make it easy for him to grip her hips. Guide her closer.

His fingers fumbled with the condom, nearly dropping it. Hell, he'd never been this torn up and out of control, out-of-his-mind turned on by a woman before. But she was warm and willing, and so ready to spread her legs for him. It was all he could do to look at her bent over like that....

Thoughts incinerating in spontaneous combustion, he cupped her breasts, thumbs tracing her tight nipples while he slid himself inside her. Slow. Easy.

Her moan filled the cabin, drowning out any noise from the engine. She was slick and hot, dripping with readiness, and she was all his. Possessiveness speared through him, making him hold tighter, his fingers squeezing her breasts together as he drew her body back to his with each deep thrust.

Her skin glistened in the half light with a sheen of sweat, her thighs flexing in time with his. She possessed such strength, such stamina, and yet he couldn't help but think how delicate the rope of her spine looked as she bent and arched with each aching movement. Releasing her breasts, he smoothed his hands around to her back, rubbing lightly over her shoulders. He gathered up her hair in one hand, winding the long length around his palm.

All the better to see you with, my dear.

The significance of the big bad wolf in his head right now wasn't lost on him. He wanted a taste of Vanessa. A bite.

She arched against him with a slow sweep of her

body, her hips fitting snugly to his as she steadied herself on the seat's headrest. One arm reached back to loop about his neck, drawing him closer. Drawing them closer.

He would never hurt her, damn it. Never let any more of his personal demons touch her. This time—with her—he wouldn't fail.

Bending to kiss the salty skin of her shoulder, he lost himself in the steady rocking of her hips, the rhythmic slide of her strong, lean body against his. The taste of her nourished him in a way nothing else ever had, the scent of her filling his nostrils until the need to make her come became his sole focus and priority.

Reaching behind him, he groped for the vial he'd set on the media cabinet along with his pants. He hadn't mentioned that he'd brought it along, not wanting her to think he was some kind of perv for indulging his sexual fantasies while they chased carjackers around New York.

But now, he uncorked the bottle while he kissed her, carefully warding off his own throbbing need. His fingers armed with a few drops of the oil they'd used the night before, he tossed the bottle aside and touched her between her legs.

She bucked against him, gasping in surprise as the tingling heat dripped down her slick folds. His fingers sizzled, too, from the liquid, and he used them to massage the moisture into her sex.

Her fingernails clenched his neck, scratching lightly

as the first wave of a shuddering orgasm wracked through her. He didn't break his rhythm, his touch guided by the pulsing sensations he could feel both inside and outside her.

His own climax slammed through him then, the force of it spinning through him until his knees buckled. He guided them down to the seats. Cradling Vanessa in his lap as they half fell, half sprawled into the leather, their bodies sealed together by sex and sweat and so much more.

If only Vanessa would see it.

He held onto her, not ready to let her go even though the plane had started to descend. The angle of the plane accounted for part of the reason his knees had given out.

"You cheated." Her breathless voice didn't sound unhappy about the fact.

"Yeah?" He swiped a lock of her hair from her forehead, knowing they'd need to get dressed soon. "How do you figure?"

"You brought along a sensual aid." She slid away from him, reaching for her shirt as the lights from the city below became more visible out the windows. "Not that I minded, of course. It was just a bit…unexpected."

"You give me all the time I want with you naked, and I promise I'll give you the best sex of your life with no toys in sight." He would find a way to have that with her, to talk Miss Independent into letting all her barriers down. "Tonight I was under time constraints."

He stepped into his pants as he watched her dress, already regretting the loss of access to her body.

"I hate to tell you this, but toys are very recreational."
She smiled as she rebraided her hair.

"Don't get used to it." He smiled back at her, looking forward to the challenge of having his way with her
again. "Next time will be on my terms."

13

IF ALEC'S TERMS INVOLVED the mini-mansion he kept in East Hampton, Vanessa told herself she would have to say no. Bad enough she'd been seduced by a jet. She couldn't be swayed by the two-story beach house he referred to as a cottage.

Sinking down into a lounge chair on his patio overlooking the water, Vanessa reminded herself that when she'd gone into law enforcement she hadn't cared about any of the superficial trappings Alec's lifestyle maintained. Still didn't. But the view over the Atlantic at this time of night could sure turn a woman's head, even if she'd take more satisfaction out of locking up criminals than testing her rusty financial-analyst skills on the stock market.

Cranking up the flame on a hurricane lamp Alec had lit on a wrought-iron patio table before he took a walk down the beach to look around, Vanessa warmed her hands by the blaze. The spring weather had been warm this week, but the breeze blowing in off the ocean chilled her now the same way it had from the moment the stairs to the Cessna had been lowered, ending her time alone with Alec.

He'd arranged for a car to meet them at the airport when he'd called for the pilot. Or perhaps that had been part of the benefit he paid for with the air-management company who provided him with pilots and serviced his plane wherever it happened to land. Either way, a driver had been waiting at the tiny municipal landing strip, and they'd arrived at the beach house a few minutes later.

They hadn't spoken much. Mostly, Vanessa thought, out of deference to their driver who shuttled them around in a Lincoln without a formal partition between the front and back. But even when they'd arrived at the house, they'd gone their own ways after Alec had pointed out the kitchen and a bathroom. They'd each made phone calls, Vanessa to Wes and Alec to heaven-only-knew who. Friends? Enemies? Donata the mistress Vanessa really didn't want to meet? He'd mentioned putting his own resources to use for scaring up a paper trail to implicate his partner, but she couldn't be sure what sort of resources Alec had in mind. Despite the beach mini-mansion and the jet that both proved he made a very successful living in real-estate development, she found it hard to envision him as anything but a loner. He seemed too intense and possibly a little too dangerous for polite company.

As she listened to the waves roll up the beach, she assured herself it didn't matter where he'd gone. She needed to scavenge some semblance of personal space and distance from the man anyhow. Not an easy feat to accomplish when they jumped each other every time they were alone together.

Her whole life seemed to be spinning out of control, and getting naked on an airplane only proved how much she'd lost it. Even now she couldn't put Alec far from her mind since the most unexpected places on her body burned from the light friction of his bristly cheek. Her neck. Her hip. Just above one breast.

Not a chance she'd forget about Alec anytime soon, but maybe once they found enough evidence to put his partner away along with the guy's slimeball nephew, Alec could go back to flying around the East Coast to monitor his real-estate development sites and she could return to...

Feeling nothing?

A sharp wind blew in off the water, wavering the lamp flame right through the glass globe and chilling her to the bone. She debated picking up her phone and re-treating inside when a dark shape took form down the beach.

Fingers moving automatically to the gun at her waist, she wondered how many of Alec's enemies already knew he'd resurfaced in the Hamptons.

"The lights are on at Donata's place." Alec's voice carried on the wind as he stalked closer, a dark shape growing bigger until at last he arrived in the ring of light around the patio table. "You ready to take a ride over there?"

What was the worst that could happen? She'd con-firm her own fears that Donata possessed the glittering lifestyle Vanessa could never aspire to on a cop's paycheck? Or was she just worried that a woman who signed herself as "Your Pussy" would embrace the kind of blatant sexuality Alec seemed to seek in bed?

"I'm game." Shoving to her feet, she pocketed her phone, refusing to allow some bogus sexual insecurity to rule her choices when it came to her job. "You can see her house but you can't walk to it?" She'd never even considered that he might have gone over to Donata's alone.

"It's down the road about a mile, but the beach curves around as you head east, so there's a good view of the houses that way." He extinguished the flame, throwing them back into the dark, causing her to stumble just a little.

Come to think of it, that was pretty much how she always felt about Alec and the whole sex issue. She knew her way around a gun and a police computer, but put her next to an attractive man and she might as well be stumbling around in the dark.

"You okay?" His hands somehow found her, his arm sliding around her waist to guide her forward off the patio and through the night. "My social interactions have been limited to contractors and teenagers for the past six months, and even then, most conversational attempts are crammed between the noise of hammers and circulating saws over at the rec center. Sorry if I've got the social aptitude of a primate."

His arm around her made her feel better than any attempt at etiquette, but she didn't think she needed to share that with him. Not when she was planning to maintain some distance before things got too complicated between them.

"I'm fine." She kept pace with him as they crossed a narrow walk to the driveway, her eyes adjusting to the dark as she followed him into a garage designed like a Cape Cod–style house. "How did you ever maintain your anonymity while converting those old buildings into the center? Didn't you run into any of the same contractors you normally work with?"

He took a set of keys off a Peg-Board on one wall and pressed the remote for a vehicle that looked like a huge SUV. A digital beeping sound bounced off the cement floor as the doors unlocked. Alec opened the passenger-side door and held out his hand for her to step up inside.

A Land Rover. The recreational vehicle of choice for guys who could afford a Cessna.

"I used all new companies this time and hired them out under the Al Perez name. Paying in cash prevents a lot of questions, so it wasn't a problem and it gave me a chance to meet some different people. I found a few good guys I'll be working with again, and a few that I won't. No real surprises there."

He started the vehicle and shifted into reverse before placing a steadying hand on her seat as he turned around to see behind him.

"Will you put any more time into the rec center now that you're going to reclaim your stake in McPherson?"

She'd wondered about that since he'd seemed so at home teaching those kids how to defend themselves.

Alec slowed the Land Rover to a stop at the end of his driveway and waited for an oncoming car.

"Definitely. Hell, I need to stay connected to those kids or I won't be able to teach them anything. They can sense when you're only showing up to earn a paycheck. Maybe once things get back to normal and I can edge Vercelli out of the company, I'll be able to tighten up the real-estate business and spend some more time at the rec center. I can hire an administrator and get things fully functional."

The rightness of the choice settled over her. Pleased her. A man like Alec could make a deeper difference than any superficial urban renewal program.

"You never told me why you think your partner turned on you." She'd asked him earlier tonight, on the airstrip. "We got distracted before we could talk about that on the plane."

She didn't bring it up to sound suggestive. She'd just meant to remind this close-mouthed man that he'd already agreed to talk to her about this. She could see the heat in his eyes even in the soft illumination from the dashboard lights.

"Yes, we did." He didn't touch her. Didn't move to tempt her. "And as I recall we made an agreement about the next time we're together."

His utter stillness made her realize he'd never *done* anything to draw her eye, to inspire this kind of heat.

The ache of need she felt had been rooted in the most instinctive physical attraction from the start. Yet instead of diminishing the attraction, that revelation only validated it for her. She didn't want him for his mini-mansion or his toys. Not the Cessna. Not the mile-high orgasms. She wanted the self-defense instructor as much as—more than?—the real-estate mogul, admiring his faith in the kids he taught even while the cynical part of her wrote off the effort as crazy. Dangerous.

"Are you trying to distract me from this question?" The thought occurred to her as she shoved aside the bout of lust. "Because this makes two times you've sidetracked me when the topic came up."

"I'm not the one doing the distracting." He eased the vehicle out onto the darkened street, his hand falling away from her seat as he drove along the county route linking tightly packed beach properties in an area where every square inch of sand was prime real estate. "And I don't think there's any great mystery about why Vercelli wants me out of the company. The trouble has been brewing with us for years, I just hoped if I ignored it long enough it would go away. Stupid approach, but it seemed easier than breaking up our company and potentially ticking off a lot of clients."

"What kind of trouble did the two of you have?" Vanessa stared out the window, searching for hints of the houses that lurked behind security fences and thick shrubbery barriers.

She'd heard many of the residents out this way only

lived here part of the year, making some of the communities ghost towns on weekdays or during the school year. The reputation seemed to apply tonight. Every now and then she spied a hint of lit fountains or swimming pools, but for the most part, she could discern only the sprawling rooftops of the three-story homes that made even Alec's mini-mansion look conservative.

"Mark's been pressuring me to bring my uncle into the business for years, and he stepped up the pressure about a year ago, though who knows why since we're making great money without any of the guaranteed contracts that go along with Sergio's business."

He drove slowly, just barely crawling up the street. Probably because Donata's house was too damn close to his.

"Maybe he was having financial problems?" Although it seemed shortsighted to draw that kind of criminal element into a successful business.

"Or maybe he just wanted a chance to carry a gun." Alec rolled his eyes as he drummed his fingers against the steering wheel. "Vercelli was always a little too impressed with my family's ties to crime. The first time I ever met him over a keg at a college party he was quoting *The Godfather.* Later he graduated to *Goodfellas,* but he didn't get any more of a clue."

"Yet you were close enough friends to start a company together." She couldn't imagine working with people she didn't respect.

Not a problem at her job.

"He's good with people." Alec seemed content to leave it at that as he turned the wheel and pulled into a private driveway. But then, as he shut off the ignition, he smiled at her across the Land Rover's front seat. "Me? I tend to scare people or put them off because I'm not a big talker. But Mark puts people at ease because he's Joe Social. He doesn't know squat about land development, but he can close a deal."

"And he closed deals for you for years and then one day he decides to pull the rug out from underneath you with a visit to the cops?" Squinting into the darkness, she took in the lines of the house that belonged to the mobster's mistress. "I don't get it. Why the change?"

"Damned if I know." He pocketed the keys and pointed to the beach cottage in front of them, a rambling one-story clapboard affair that defied architectural description thanks to a century's worth of add-ons. Rooms sprawled out in every direction along with tacked-on screened porches. "But maybe she will."

Vanessa didn't understand why he thought so, but she followed his lead and opened the door to let herself out of the Land Rover. Maybe she'd just save her questions for their midnight house call.

Making her way up the stone path to the front door encrusted in seashells, Vanessa could see the house predated Alec's place a mile up the road. In a stretch of beach where big, showy homes rubbed shoulders with older dwellings built on a much smaller scale, Donata's residence strayed to the less grand. The simple bungalow architecture and painted siding would have seemed charming on a country lake, but in the Hamptons the house looked like part of a bygone era.

Alec ignored the doorbell outlined in a scallop-shaped plaster molding and rapped on the clapboard siding instead.

"Come here often?" Vanessa muttered under her breath, still half wishing she hadn't made the visit with him in the first place.

Alec turned dark eyes on her under the porch light, allowing just enough heat in his gaze to remind her how much he wanted *her.* Only her.

She felt that stare of his clear down to her toes, the slow, sensual thrill of it giving her the urge to fan herself.

The door opened in the middle of their steamy exchange. Only the person on the other side wasn't the sex-crazed woman Vanessa expected. Instead, a tall, wiry guy with glasses stood framed in the doorway, his expression quickly twisting into a mask of rage.

"Sergio?" Alec's stance shifted. Straightened.

Vanessa didn't have time to go for her gun. The guy on the step charged out of the house like a bull closing in on a red flag.

"You goddamn son of a—" Sergio's curses were punctuated by a feminine scream within the house, but Vanessa kept her eyes trained on Alec and his uncle, who'd either made a jailbreak or had been released on bail since his drug bust the night before.

Alec lowered his shoulder before Sergio hit him, sheltering his body from the worst of the blow. They crashed to the stone pathway leading up to the house and then half fought, half rolled their way into the wet grass.

"Alec!" The anguished feminine cry from the porch steps didn't distract Vanessa as she hurried after them, gun drawn. She wouldn't use the 9 mm with Alec locked in the guy's pissed-off grip, but God help him if he let Alec go.

Fear pulsing through her, she flashed her badge with her other hand and shouted at the rolling tumbleweed of arms and legs while fists flew.

"Stop! NYPD, you're under arrest." Cramming the badge back in her jacket pocket, she figured she'd done her duty to alert him to her presence.

If anything happened to Alec...

"You brought a cop with you?" Sergio's muffled shout came from underneath the pile and Vanessa noticed it looked as if Alec had regained the upper hand despite Sergio's fingers around his throat. "That's some kind of freaking loyalty, you double-dealing dumb ass."

His foot kicked out, knocking over a statue of a fat cherub keeping vigil over a bed of purple irises.

"We're here to see—" Alec's voice sounded strained from the pressure to his throat, but then he managed to slam Sergio's head against the stone path, forcing his attacker's fingers loose "—Donata. Not you, you crazy bastard."

He freed himself from his uncle and stood up while Vanessa kept her gun trained on Sergio, her heart still slamming with leftover fear for Alec.

She never should have denied Alec's request to go to the police now that he had his disks to back up his story. Damning her need for evidence at the risk of his life, she stepped closer to Sergio.

This charade of an investigation would end right now. Training her weapon on the gangster, she planned to make herself very clear to the man.

"Don't move, or I'll shoot."

ALEC SWIPED THE GRASS from the back of his head, hoping he could talk Vanessa out of arresting Sergio quite yet. But she didn't look like she was in any mood for conversation.

His uncle's groan a few feet away made Alec tense, especially since he could practically feel Vanessa tense, too. How had he ended up this in-tune to her, this keyed-in to how she thought?

The realization reminded him how important she'd become in a short amount of time.

"I'd take her at her word, Serg." He played it cool, not wanting to bust Vanessa's cop groove or mess with her concentration when she looked so utterly focused on her target. "I've seen her in action and I'm pretty sure she could take you down with or without the gun."

"Is that a fact?" Donata stepped off the porch toward them, lingering just close enough to the circle of light to silhouette her body underneath a floor-length dressing gown. The hip-jutting pose she struck looked a bit too calculated to be an accident, and despite the mild spring weather, she had to be freezing with the ocean breeze blowing up the shore. "Come to think of it, she does look a little rough around the edges."

Alec's eyes flicked over to Vanessa but she never gave any sign of reaction. Instead, he saw hints of the cool ice princess who'd walked into his rec center and flipped him on his ass, as Vanessa shouted back to Donata.

"Because I'm not flitting around the front yard in my nightie?" A slow smile spread across Vanessa's face while she kept the gun trained on Sergio. "I'll leave the pneumonia to you, thanks just the same. Besides, I'd rather not attract any attention from pea-brained mob lackeys."

Sergio groaned louder, possibly to cover up the name Donata chose to call Vanessa. Yeah, this was going really well. Alec turned his back on Donata as she huffed her way back inside the house and slammed the door.

Just as well. Alec lowered himself to sit on the front-porch steps between a few more cherub statues, while Vanessa watched over Sergio on the walkway. Alec's throat ached like hell from where his uncle had jammed a thumb into his windpipe. Sergio was approaching fifty, but he worked out and he'd always been a big guy. Alec could take him, but he'd be willing to bet there were plenty of thirty-year-old guys who couldn't. Of course, it helped that Serg had probably mixed it up in his line of work a few times.

Experience was still the best teacher.

"Look, we came out here to get some answers from Donata about what the hell is going on with your people following me."

"I'll bet that's all you want from Donata, you mother—"

"Hey. Would you watch your mouth if you want to spend the night in your own bed? I don't think my friend the detective is going to be moved to let you off the hook if you're spewing filth like a backed-up toilet. You hear me?" At least Vanessa hadn't arrested his uncle yet. Alec wanted his answers now. Tonight. "And for the record, I never laid a finger on Donata."

More swearing ensued, followed by a heavy sigh. "Can I at least get up off the god—the ground?"

Vanessa shifted her stance, backing up a step. "You just take it slow. Easy. Hands where I can see them. And don't even think about standing up."

Sergio must have been tired because he didn't argue, settling for giving her the evil eye through his dark-rimmed glasses as he sat up. He liked to brag that his vision had gone bad because he'd read too many books in his youth, sort of a self-styled know-it-all. But Alec happened to know he wore glasses just because his grandfather once predicted he'd be as dumb as his father before him, a curse Sergio somehow figured he'd beat by wearing spectacles.

Sergio's solution only seemed to confirm his grand-pappy's point.

"My people aren't following you." Sergio adjusted the glasses on his nose, which Alec now noticed was bleeding. "Where do you get these dumb-ass ideas?"

Alec glared a warning, grateful Vanessa still had the gun on him. "Oh, I don't know. Maybe because you threatened to kill me six months ago and then turned my partners against me."

"That's bullshit and you know it." He swiped his shirtsleeve across his bloody nose. "Your partners are as crooked as the day is long. McPherson ripped me off last summer when I asked him to install a new shower in Donata's house. You think he could do a favor for a friend?"

"He's not a contractor, Serg." His uncle had probably asked Alec to fix twenty different things in the past ten years, everything from installing a new roof to replacing a furnace. He'd never gotten it through his head that Alec just bought the land and planned the spaces to build. He didn't build them himself. "I keep telling you, we hire out jobs like that. And if you weren't following me six months ago, then who was leaving all the threatening messages on my machine and sabotaging my job sites?"

"Well that was me, obviously." Sergio shrugged as if it was no big deal. "I had to convince you to stay away from my girl." He peered around Alec to the vacant porch and then shouted through the night. "Donata! Get your butt back out here."

"Quite the charmer, aren't you?" Vanessa shifted positions again to give herself a clear view of both the front door and Sergio.

Smart woman.

Alec stared at her a moment longer, reassuring himself she was okay. She'd had a hell of a twenty-four hours and not much sleep, but she looked steadier now with her gun in hand and her posture utterly straight than she had in her car earlier when she'd told him about her sister.

No wonder she functioned so well in a crisis. She'd already survived the most frightening kind.

That strength of hers was what called him to her, attracted him in a way no other woman had before. Alec's convoluted life called for a lot of strength, too, and he couldn't help but admire someone who could breeze into his world of divided loyalties and divided identities and still come away with her head screwed on damn straight.

The front door banged open, revealing Donata in the same silk robe and matching nightgown she'd been cavorting around the yard in earlier. Alec wondered why he'd ever bothered trying to help a woman who was that oblivious to making smart choices for herself. As she clicked her way down the walkway in high-heel slippers complete with fluffy fur at the toes, Alec decided she couldn't be a day older than Vanessa. She was an attractive woman with chin-length platinum-blond hair, her petite frame padded with lush curves. Alec had never understood why she'd stuck around with his uncle for nearly a year.

"I was getting you an ice pack, baby." She made kissy faces at Sergio while she tossed him a bag of frozen green beans. "For your nose."

Vanessa made a threatening noise that sounded like a low growl. "Not smart to toss things into my firing range. Bad, bad idea."

Sergio clamped the frozen vegetables to his big mug of a face. "Donata, tell Alec I was only threatening him to keep us together." He turned to Alec and shrugged. "You and me—we're family. I wouldn't whack my own sister's kid."

Unless Donata convinced her lover that she'd slept with Alec.

Alec watched her go to Sergio's side now, her white gown dragging through the damp grass as she entered Vanessa's firing range and knelt by the guy.

Did the woman have no sense? Or were all her manipulative games part of some larger scheme?

Vanessa angled back, accommodating her bigger target now that the two of them knelt together. "I'd like to remind you that Alec has proof of these threats filed with my precinct. Harassing him any further will jeopardize your bail."

"Sore subject, lady." Sergio dropped the beans as he slid his arms around Donata and shoved her closer. "Those DEA guys and the DA must think I've got cash coming out my ass for what they asked in blood money to let me out of jail today."

Alec was in no mood to watch Donata kiss up to the

man she swore kept her in fear for her life. He'd had enough lies and deception to last him at least another decade or two.

"Look, we'll get out of here if you can just tell me what's up between you and my partners." He figured he'd keep the question nice and open-ended to see how his uncle tackled it.

"That money-grubbing McPherson won't be back around since he knows I'm pissed about the shower he installed for a boatload of cash. But Vercelli is another story since he's the latest bum to come sniffing around Donata." This time Sergio's grip on his girlfriend looked a little less endearing, a little more threatening.

Shit.

Alec wouldn't let himself get sucked back into their problems. He stole a look at Vanessa, who seemed to be keeping an eye on Sergio's hands, too.

"Serg, Mark's married and I've never known him to cheat on his wife. I think you're worrying for nothing." His partner might be a lot of things, but he wasn't a player.

"Tell that to Donata who's stuck fighting him off every time I go into the city. My neighbors will tell you how many times his truck has been here in the last month." Sergio swung his glare from Alec to Vanessa. "I'm going inside and taking my girl to bed, and the two of you can go screw yourselves if you don't like it. I've talked to enough guns today between the cops and the feds."

Vanessa never lowered her weapon, but she did back toward the Land Rover. "Nice to meet you, too, Sergio. And don't forget what I told you about staying away from Alec."

Sergio forced a sarcastic grin before he walked into the house. "That Alec is quite a guy isn't he?" He cursed under his breath and pried open the front door. "Why don't you spend a little less time chasing down innocent guys with guns and a little more time keeping my nephew busy in the sack so he stays away from my girl?"

Alec opened the passenger door of the Land Rover to help Vanessa inside, thinking that was the only semi-intelligent thing his uncle had ever had to say.

He turned to share the joke with Vanessa when he touched her arm to help her inside. The words on his lips dried right up when he realized that cool, calm and collected Vanessa was shaking.

14

"YOUR UNCLE IS LUCKY he's stayed alive this long in his line of work." Vanessa levered herself up into the vehicle, hoping Alec wouldn't call her on the fact that she trembled like a kid on her first trip to juvie. "No offense, but he doesn't seem slick enough to keep pace with the low-profile crooks running the mob these days."

She reached for the door handle, ready to leave this place far behind them. Alec must have been on the same page since he shut her inside and stalked around to the driver's side.

"You okay?" His voice rumbled in time with the engine coming to life.

"I'm fine." Never been better. Just coming to terms with the ten years Sergio had knocked off her life when he tackled Alec into a bed of irises.

He remained quiet for a long moment as he backed out of the driveway and headed toward his beach house a mile up the road. Vanessa cracked the window to allow the ocean air inside, inhaling deeply to settle her frazzled nerves.

"You don't seem okay," he pressed a minute later as

they rolled to a stop in front of his house and waited for a break in oncoming traffic. "I hope he didn't rattle you, Vanessa, because I swear I'd never let him get near you."

She resisted the urge to pound her head on the dashboard as he crossed the road and pulled into the garage. Could he be that clueless?

"You think I was scared for *myself?*" Frustration steamed through her as he clicked off the ignition. "Damn it, Alec, I had a gun. I also happen to have more training than ninety percent of New York's police force, so I didn't think for a moment that Sergio and his bag of frozen green beans posed a threat to me."

Alec was a smart guy, but even with that intelligence on his side, it took a surprisingly long moment before realization dawned in his expression.

"You were scared for me?"

Bingo. "I get a little frazzled any time someone is in danger on my watch. You heard me today when I talked about my sister's accident, right? I can't stand the idea of missing something, of being oblivious again during a surprise attack. And let me tell you, I wasn't prepared to see Sergio there tonight."

His silence went on for an uncomfortably long time.

"What?" Impatience nipped her along with just a little bit of self-consciousness. Had he read something into her fears? Some emotion she hadn't fully grappled with yet? "Cops aren't allowed to be scared sometimes?"

He shook his head slowly. "Not hardly. Fear is

healthy in your line of work. But you were shaking just now like a Chihuahua in winter."

"Not when it counted." She'd held her gun steady, damn the man, and that's all that really mattered. Except now that they'd slept together he probably deserved more of an explanation than her knee-jerk defensive posturing. "But you're right, I don't usually get that shaken up in your everyday average street tussle."

He waited, patient and unmoving in the darkened car inside his garage. The setting seemed an unlikely spot to trade confidences, but the inky blackness made it marginally easier.

Taking a deep breath, she offered what little understanding she had of her unwieldy emotions. "I don't know what happened last night in bed—okay, technically I *do* know, but there was more to it than just the barrage of orgasms."

"For me, too."

His quiet words threw her. He probably meant it to reassure her, but if anything, the confession only made her more rattled. If it hadn't been about just sex for him, what *had* it been about?

Not ready to think about those unsettling thoughts, she shared what she understood. "I've been switched off inside for a long time. Ever since my sister's accident, actually. And somehow, between the carjacking and the wild sex last night, I seem to have gotten switched back on. Kind of like I'm feeling everything around me firsthand now, whereas up until then, I'd been experiencing life through a veil. No deep pain. But then again, no real big joys either."

"That's because we touched each other." He shifted closer; she could sense him coming closer even if she couldn't see him in the pitch-black car interior. "Inside."

A whisper of fear wiggled up her spine, but it wasn't the kind that Sergio's fists inspired. This had more to do with insecurity and uncertainty, a fear she could never find any sort of future with a man like Alec.

Still, fear or no fear, she suspected he was coming closer to kiss her. And she definitely didn't want to stop him. More than anything, she wanted his taste on her lips, his hands all over her body. Then she wouldn't have to think. She could simply feel.

A ringing in her ears kept her from falling into him. An annoying, repetitive ringing.

Emanating from her jacket pocket.

Damn.

"I'd better take this just in case it's Wes." She pulled out her phone and flicked open the case to read the caller's number by the dim green light in the digital screen. "It's my sister."

She answered automatically, trusting Alec to recognize why she would need to speak to Gena at any time of the day or night. Even if they'd been two seconds from kissing.

"Hello?" She blinked from the brightness as Alec opened his door and stepped out of the vehicle.

"Don't hello me." Her sister's brusque voice launched directly into conversation. No time for niceties in her hurry-up world. "I stopped by the precinct tonight since I knew you'd be on duty."

"I called in sick." She accepted Alec's hand as he opened her door and helped her out of the Land Rover. Where did he get such nice—though totally unnecessary—manners when his uncle seemed like such an obnoxious pig of a man?

"Wes told me he's worried about you. Where are you and what gives?"

"I'm not at liberty to discuss that right now." Vanessa allowed herself to be tugged along the narrow walkway into Alec's house. "But I promise I'll give you a call back tomorrow and explain everything."

After she'd thought of a good cover story.

"Did I just hear the sound of crashing waves in the background, Vanessa?" Gena's voice sounded just like their grandmother's when Nana decided to be stern with them.

An unexpected smile tugged at Vanessa's lips as she dropped into a kitchen chair at the tiny café table across from Alec's refrigerator. Beneath Gena's brusque tone, Vanessa could make out the sounds of an old Earth, Wind and Fire tune. One of their favorites when they'd been kids.

A million years ago.

"Let's make a deal. I won't ask you why you've got out Nana's collection of old 45s tonight if you don't ask

me why I took a sick day to spend at the beach, okay?"
Vanessa knew her sister hated to be seen as sentimental.
She equated nostalgia with weakness—an idea she'd
picked up somewhere along the way during her recovery.

An idea Vanessa usually shared, until recently. God,
how had she morphed into Miss Emotional all of a
sudden?

On the other end of the phone, Gena sniffed. A
haughty sniff? Or was she more upset than she let on?

"Fine. But I need to hear from you before I leave the
office tomorrow, or I'm calling that know-it-all lieutenant of yours and spilling the beans that you're not really sick."

On Gena's end of the phone, Earth, Wind and Fire
faded into Donna Summer. No question, her sister was
having a bad night.

"I promise to call." Vanessa didn't know what she'd
be able to tell her sibling interrogator then, but she'd
come up with something better when she wasn't reel-
ing from too many emotions churned up by seeing Alec
go fist-to-fist with a gangster. "Although I can't imagine you'd suffer Russell Durant on the phone long
enough to rat me out."

Her sister had gone enough rounds with the lieutenant in court cases over the past two years to cement an of-
ficial rivalry. Russ liked to call her Attila behind her back.

"To keep you safe, I can handle him. Besides, he's
less insufferable when he's not on the witness stand."

Russell Durant? News to her since Gena usually went out of her way to avoid him.

Sensing strange things afoot in Gena's world, between the Motown-fest and the relaxed stance in regard to her sworn enemy, Vanessa figured they were due for a visit as soon as she made sure Alec's partner was behind bars with no chance for bail.

"Maybe we can go to lunch this week. Pedicures are on me this time."

They never actually ate meals on their lunch breaks, using the time instead for the girly stuff they didn't get to indulge in with anyone else in their male-dominated workplaces. Lunch had become a code word for girl talk.

"Maybe. We should go visit Nana."

"Definitely." Their grandmother was coping with the early stages of Alzheimer's, but on her lucid days she kept the nursing staff hopping at her care facility by applying her repair skills to whatever she could find. Her specialty was scamming extra cable stations by working some sort of illegal magic on the wiring. "Night, Gena."

"Take care of yourself, girl." She disconnected, abruptly ending the seventies disco soundtrack running in Vanessa's ear.

"Everything okay?" Alec's voice startled her a few feet away, his body hidden behind a pantry door where he seemed to be rooting around for something. He emerged with a soup can in each hand. "I don't have much to eat since I haven't stocked up in six months, but there's chicken noodle and minestrone."

"Who can eat when your partner could be headed this way to try and take you out?" She hadn't been thinking clearly this afternoon when he'd seen Vercelli talking to the guy who'd stolen Alec's car the night before. "I screwed up not letting you go to the precinct today like you suggested. You deserve police protection."

"I don't need police protection now that I know where the threat is coming from." He set the cans down by the stove and stalked closer. "I can handle Mark."

"But what if he hires some drugged-up psycho like his nephew again?" She shuddered at the memory of the carjackers, hating the unpredictability factor of criminals on drugs. Bad enough people committed crimes that endangered everyone else. But when they did it under the influence of something that made them out of touch with reality, that sucked all the worse. Good cops died that way. Innocent bystanders were injured. Or worse.

"Then I'll deal with it when the time comes, but I'm not going to borrow trouble for weeks while I wait and see what their next move will be." Pulling her to her feet, he skimmed his hands down her arms. "I can't change the fact that I'm related to Sergio, or that being part of his family puts me into some awkward situations with other people around me, but I can damn well change the way I relate to him and all the trouble he brings into my life."

"Is he the reason you carry a gun?" She didn't know many people outside law enforcement who owned a weapon. Alec had at least two.

"Construction sites are notorious places for crime. It seems safer to have the weapon and not use it than to not have it the one time I might need some backup."

"Makes sense." And it fit with what she knew of Alec, all the little facets of him coming together to form a more complete image in her mind.

"You trust me, don't you?" Tipping her chin up to look at him, she met his gaze filled with more complex emotions than she was ready to see, let alone understand.

Still, she could reassure him on this much, at least.

"I trust you more than I trust some of the guys on my own force." She knew the people in her own precinct were solid, honest. But in the past, she'd worked with other cops she wouldn't put her complete faith in. "I'll never forget the way you stayed by me when those dirtballs hauled me out of your car. You put yourself in the line of fire to be there for me."

And it wasn't even his job.

The air in the kitchen grew warm, intimate. Alec's magnetic stare drew her in even when the warnings in her head told her that to continue this conversation would be risky for them both.

"You mean something to me, Vanessa. I know you don't want to think about that yet, but I'm not the kind of guy to hold back when I want more. No more hiding for me."

His lips hovered closer, persuading her to lean into him even when she knew she ought to pull away. Gather what little sanity she had left where he was concerned.

Her lips brushed his and just that barest of touches sent flashes of light exploding behind her eyelids. She'd never been a superstitious woman, but Alec's touch wrought something damn close to magic as far as she was concerned.

Logically, she understood he wanted more from this relationship, but this newfound heat inside her urged her to simply indulge the pleasure they found together and worry about how to make sense of it later. When her job wasn't on the line along with Alec's life. First they'd make it through this, then they'd figure out how to cope with the fallout.

"I need a shower first." She mumbled the words aloud as soon as she committed to the fact that they were going to be together again. No way could she sleep tonight without holding him in her arms, reassuring herself he was okay after his mobster uncle had tried to take him down. "You can join me if you want."

WOULD THIS WOMAN ever stop surprising him?

Alec figured she'd want to talk about her sister, or the case, or his plan of action now that he'd advertised his return to the Hamptons as loudly as possible. But no. Vanessa Torres, kick-ass cop, wanted a shower.

He wouldn't dream of disappointing her.

"You remember what I told you on the plane earlier?" He'd been expecting her to keep her distance, not jump in with both feet. "Next time we get naked, there's no holding back."

He angled back to gauge her expression but couldn't get a good read on her face. Intrigued? Scared? Possibly a little of both.

No matter. He'd never been the kind of guy to take a lover just for kicks. If they were going to keep being together, it had to mean something.

He knew what it meant to him.

"Sure I remember." She backed away, a wicked glint in her eyes. "You were trying to take charge of whatever this is that's happening between us, but I have the feeling this connection of ours won't be strong-armed into submission just because you want it to be."

His feet followed her automatically as she wound her way out of the kitchen and through the living area.

"Wait a minute." He hurried to catch up, wondering how she knew right where to find the best shower in the house. He'd made a point of not pointing out his bedroom when they'd arrived. "If you think I'm going to forget about this just because you start distracting me with sex talk about submission—" holy hell "—you are very much mistaken."

"Who says submission and sex have a damn thing to do with one another?" Still, she continued to smile as she strode right into his bedroom and whipped off her jacket. Her tank top.

Leaving her clad in a dark satin bra that perfectly molded itself to the natural shape of her breasts.

She paused just before the door to the master bathroom, pivoting on one barefoot heel to face him.

"Coming?"

He shouldn't have been surprised at her choice of word given her mood. She looked even more dangerous now clad in her sleek, silky bra than she had in his rec center, staring down at him with a gymnasium full of would-be street thugs by her side.

"Hell yeah, I'm coming." He wouldn't let her off with just a few orgasms and a bunch of provocative words. He'd glimpsed what they could be like together, a deeper connection that would take them through years instead of days, and he didn't plan on trading that in for a few short-term sex games. Tugging his shirt over his head, he double-checked the house security alarms on the remote by his bed. He could go for a few rounds of whatever Vanessa had in mind, but only if he could guarantee they'd stay safe long enough to enjoy it.

A low whistle from the bathroom hastened his pace. He brought the remote with him as he followed Vanessa inside, where she was already turning on the shower.

"Not in a million years would I have pegged you for something so hedonistic." She stepped out of her jeans as her gaze lingered on the multiple showerheads positioned at varying heights along one wall of the open shower.

"It's my one indulgence."

"Right after the Cessna." She held her hand under the spray from the nearest nozzle, her fingers drumming into the water.

"That's business." He shut the bathroom door behind him, enclosing them in the safety of the interior room with no windows. Not that he was worried about Vercelli showing up here. Yet.

It would take the guy a couple of hours to drive out from the city, and chances were he wouldn't have heard about Alec resurfacing until an hour ago at the earliest.

"And this is pleasure." She tipped her head back into the spray, not bothering to remove her bra or panties. "I like the way you think, Messina."

He liked the way her undergarments molded to her skin the same way his hands would in another minute.

Stepping out of his clothes, he watched her reach for the soap and lather up.

"I visited Italy a few years back and stayed in this great hotel where the bathroom didn't have a shower curtain, just a big tile basin and tile walls."

"And you realized what a great view you could have if you left everything open." She ran her hands over her wet curves, her fingers slick with suds.

Creating a hell of a view.

"At the time, I just liked the idea of never seeing mildew again." Naked, he pulled a condom out of the bathroom cabinet and made his way toward her. "But now I see I was pretty damn shortsighted."

Her fingers reached for him along with the shower spray, a stream of water pulsating against his chest.

"You can look your fill tonight." She cupped his jaw, tipping his head down to hers for a kiss and an eyeful of wet and willing woman.

He tasted her with a thoroughness that left his thoughts scrambled.

"Don't think I don't know what you're doing." He cupped a breast in his palm, lifting her toward his mouth as he bent closer.

"What's that?" She arched into his kiss, her skin hot and sweet against his tongue.

He forced himself to straighten, to leave that dusky pink crest for a minute. Long enough to talk to her.

"You're trying to make me forget everything I wanted to say to you this time."

"But is it working?" Peeling off the straps of her bra from her shoulders, she leaned forward enough to allow the spray of the highest nozzle to fill the loosened cups to overflowing. She closed her eyes, as if transfixed by the wash of water over the breasts he'd rather bathe with his tongue.

"Damn right it's working." He unhooked the bra and flung it aside before imprisoning her wrists. "That's why I have to hold you still long enough to keep my head together."

His breath came fast and shallow, his fingers twitching to feel every soaking inch of her. She slid sinuous curves against him, the wet slide of her skin defying him to keep her still for long.

"There you go again with that submission idea." She licked a kiss up the side of his jaw, her teeth nipping at his ear. "What makes you think you can keep me still unless I really want to be held down?"

Good intentions streaming down the drain faster than the sudsy water, Alec told himself the quicker he spoke his mind, the quicker he could have her. Backing her against the wall, he sheltered her from a hot stream of a jet at hip level.

"Just know this. We're either in this together because we're crazy about each other, or—at least to my way of thinking—we've got no business together." He'd waited so long to be able to claim everything he wanted out in the open. He wouldn't wait around to be with her, too.

"You're putting an end to recreational sex?" Her utter stillness made him wary.

Yet, his purpose was noble. Honorable. And hell yes, it would be a lot of fun for them both.

"Only in favor of the better kind." He kissed her, gentled his hold on her wrists in an attempt to show her exactly what he had in mind. "The committed kind."

"A commitment?" Her legs wavered against his just a little. He hoped the idea turned her on as much as it lit his every freaking fire.

"We can barely keep our hands off each other." Correction, he wouldn't *ever* be able to keep his hands off her. Why not acknowledge that need and strengthen the heat between them all the more? Grazing a kiss along her shoulder, he savored the thought of something deeper. "I want you in my life, Vanessa."

Ready to show her just how much he wanted her now that he'd spoken his piece, Alec moved to turn them both into the shower spray.

Only Vanessa wasn't moving.

He glanced to her face, not sure how to read her expression, but fairly certain she didn't look like a woman who'd been propositioned with forever.

"We just met." Her words sent a trickle of cold down his spine despite the steamy blast of hot water.

"And I don't want to rush you, but I also need for you to understand my intentions go beyond sex."

"So do mine. But my other main intention is to throw your scumbag partner behind bars, and if your mobster uncle gets in my way, I plan to take him in, too." She stood perfectly still, her body grazing his in places, but somehow she seemed a million miles away. "I can't think about a commitment with someone I only just met, no matter how incredible our time together has been."

"You know how many times we've gotten naked in two days?" Frustration stomped through him, not sure how to make her understand. "Don't get me wrong. I can appreciate the appeal of a one-night stand. Possibly the lure of a next-day booty call. But continuing to hook up just for sex's sake smacks of a casualness I don't want any part of, and I don't think you do, either."

"I haven't had sex with anyone but you in years." She moved away from him, her steps rigid. Controlled. "Don't try to tell me that a little wild sex after all this time makes me some kind of skank."

"Hell no, Vanessa." How could he have botched things up this badly? "I'm packing major feelings for you, lady, and I'm pretty freaking sure I'm falling in love with you. How the hell can you turn that into me saying you're anything but phenomenal?"

She shook her head. Slowly. Awkwardly, at first. But then faster. "No. You don't even know me."

"That's BS and you know it." He pounded his fist into the tile, damning his rush to clarify their relationship. "I just wanted to be fair to you. To make sure you understood I'd gladly hand over ten more Mercedes for the chance to share something more with you. Something real. Jesus, I've been made out to be a mob guy for so long that the taint hovers over everything I do and I couldn't stand the idea of anything tainting this. Distorting your idea of me."

Shutting off the shower, he reached for a towel. He handed one to her without comment, figuring he'd damn well said enough for today.

"Alec—" She reached for him, but her hand never touched him as the peal of the remote alarm blistered through the steamy bathroom.

The house's security had been breached.

15

THE BEADS OF WATER on Vanessa's skin turned icy as the sirens all around the house blared. She sprinted into the bedroom two steps behind Alec, already tugging her clothes on. Bright white flashes blinked outside his bedroom windows as the system switched on floodlights.

"Does your system link to the local police?" She tugged her jeans on and pulled a sweater Alec handed her over her head.

"No. All this is more for show. I disconnected the link to the cop shop six months ago when I went into hiding since I didn't want every hungry skunk in search of food bringing the police out here." Dressed and .357 in hand, he moved toward the front window to look outside. "Christ. It's just Sergio's truck in the driveway."

He reached for a remote from the nightstand and stabbed a couple of buttons in quick succession to disarm the system. Quiet reigned again.

Surprised he would turn off the alarm when his visitor was a known criminal, Vanessa edged near the window. "He could be here to carry out the threats he made last winter."

"That's why I'll be armed, and I'll reactivate the system, so that if anyone else tries a door or window on the house, the light display and alarms will kick back into high gear. It may not bring the cops automatically, but eventually one of the neighbors will place a call to the police to get the system shut off." He unlocked the sash and opened the window to shout down toward a tall figure standing in a tulip bed. "What the hell are you doing here?"

"I wanted to talk to you about that rat bastard partner of yours when Donata wasn't around." Sergio stepped out of the tulips and closer to the window. "Can I come in, or what?"

Vanessa would sooner invite a serpent inside. Her fingers flexed around her weapon, wondering how Alec had put up with this kind of uncertainty his whole life. How did anyone conduct a normal existence with a criminal in the family?

"I'll come out instead." Pulling shut the window, Alec latched it before drawing all the wooden blinds and turning off what few interior lights had been turned on. "I need to at least hear what he has to say."

"Why not let the police find out?" She hated that she hadn't brought him to her precinct when he'd agreed to go with her. "You could just call the local cops and let them—"

"Bring me in for questioning?" His brow lifted, his not-so-subtle reference to her own initial attempt to haul him into the precinct reminding her why that probably wouldn't work. On paper, a guy with Alec's connections looked pretty damn suspicious.

Hurrying through the darkened house, she appreciated the sparse furnishings that kept her pathway clear as they headed toward the stairs. The simple Cape Cod–style home—albeit built on a huge scale—seemed in keeping with a man who liked his toys but could also make himself at home in a converted rec center. Luxurious and pared down at the same time.

"You think Sergio can really give us something on your partner?" She followed him down the bare hardwood stairs toward the side entrance, her body humming with adrenaline and—yes—unfulfilled desire.

"Not us. *Me*."

"You've got to be joking." She needed to be there by his side to make sure Sergio didn't decide to try anything funny. Mark Vercelli might be guilty of setting up the carjacking, but she hadn't let Sergio off the hook for making threats to Alec last winter.

"No. I need you to keep an eye on him from the inside in case he tries to get the drop on me. I don't expect any trouble. Hell, he's my uncle and I've been dealing with him for years. I know how to handle him, okay? But if there's trouble, you can call the cops while you pick him off from the kitchen window." He gestured toward the bump-out glass surrounding the breakfast nook. "Find a spot over there and I'll try to lead him around to the patio in back."

It was a solid plan, giving her no choice but to nod

agreement even though she wanted to twine her arms around his neck one more time before he went outside. A selfish urge when only a few minutes ago she'd been pushing him away—or at least, pushing away the emotions he wanted her to recognize.

And now he headed out to meet a threat that could very well be deadly.

"Alec?"

"Yeah?"

"I'll be watching every move he makes, but it you want me to act sooner, just give me the sign."

"I'll be fine. It's more important that you keep an eye peeled for Mark in case he decides to put in an appearance tonight." He leaned down to kiss her—hard—on the mouth. "Be careful."

She blinked through her fears and the swell of feelings for Alec as he turned and went outside, leaving her alone in the kitchen to get her head together.

She hadn't even given much thought to his partner showing up here. Especially not tonight. Somehow, she'd told herself all of Alec's problems were in the city, hiding in scary corners of the South Bronx, but obviously his enemies could follow him wherever he went. Trouble wasn't limited to 172nd Street, damn it.

Situating herself to one side of the large kitchen window looking out onto the patio, Vanessa settled in to watch Alec greet his uncle. With all the lights off downstairs, she figured she could allow herself a narrow sliver of glass to peer through without worrying Sergio would notice. She edged aside the wooden blinds slowly, cautiously, careful not to make a sudden movement.

Alec flicked on the exterior patio lights and then lit the same hurricane lamp on the patio table that she'd used earlier. The bright glow outdoors helped her pick out their movements more readily, the ring of light allowing her to see Sergio's elbows on the table as well as his lap beneath. Granted, his clothes were dark, but she didn't spy any glint of metal, no bulge that would suggest he had a gun nearby.

Seeing the men's mouths move in rapid exchange, she reached for the crank on the casement to open the window an inch or two. Hopefully with the crash of ocean waves behind them, Sergio would never hear the small creak of the sash as she nudged it open.

"…can't trust anybody." Sergio made wild hand gestures, his whole form brimming with caged energy. Anger. "I'm not even sure Donata is on the up-and-up with me sometimes. You know I caught her going through my drawers the other night?"

Sergio had come over here at one o'clock in the morning to discuss his fears about Donata? Vanessa wondered if he hoped to trap Alec somehow into admitting they'd had some kind of relationship.

But then again, why would a mobster waste time hashing out his girl trouble with his nephew? He sounded like a Jerry Springer episode— *My bimbo girlfriend is cheating on me!*

She swallowed a snort as she imagined tough guy

Sergio whining about his problems on daytime TV. Drawing her attention back to the conversation on the patio, she heard Alec say something about Donata probably worrying that Sergio had cheated on her.

"Maybe she was looking for lipstick stains or something."

"In my underwear drawer?" Sergio nearly busted a gut over that one before lowering his voice to confide more problems Vanessa couldn't hear.

And as much as she wanted to listen, to keep her eyes on Alec and ensure his uncle didn't make a move against him, she knew she ought to check out front to be certain Alec's partner didn't show up to catch Alec unaware.

Easing away from the window, she padded through the dark house in bare feet. Ears alert, she moved cautiously. Alec had said he'd reactivated the security system after Sergio's loud arrival so that it would go off if someone tried to come inside. But she couldn't be too careful. She wouldn't let anyone take her unaware. He'd trusted her enough to watch his back.

Refusing to let herself get rattled over that realization and everything it meant, she tightened her grip around her gun as she peered out one of the front door's sidelight windows. The yard remained quiet and still, with only Sergio's car in the driveway.

Forcing herself to keep sentinel for two endless minutes as her gaze swept the grounds for any sign of movement, she crept back through the house toward where she really wanted to be—watching over Alec.

Nothing would happen to him on her watch, damn it. She'd made it through five years on the police force without letting Gena's accident mess with her head, but now that she was protecting someone she cared about, she found it far more difficult to separate her cop instincts from her more personal fears for Alec.

Her gaze zeroed in on him as she settled into her position at the kitchen window again. He kept his attention focused on Sergio, his posture relaxed in his chair even though Vanessa could sense the tension in his shoulders, the way he bent his neck from side to side every now and again as if to relieve tension there. She admired that about him, the quiet way he took care of business.

Funny how in two days' time she already knew so much about him, knew that he would never whine about his problems to anyone else the way Sergio was still doing even now. Alec relied on himself, employing his own means to deal with the accident of birth that made him related to a gangster. And instead of running scared from his uncle's demands for kickbacks, he'd built a thriving business in spite of him—in spite of a partner who couldn't wait to get his hands dirty out of pure greed.

Alec might look dark and dangerous—who was she kidding? He *was* dark and dangerous—but inside he hid an altruistic side that built projects like the rec center. And he was the kind of guy who wouldn't leave her side even at great risk to his own neck. Vanessa knew cops who would have taken off the other night during the car-jacking. Oh, they would have excused their exit with avowals of going to get help, but bottom line, she would have been left to her own devices to fend off doped-up hoodlums.

But Alec had stayed because he possessed an old-world nobility that wouldn't let him leave another in danger. The same old-world nobility that made him honor-bound to declare feelings for a woman he was sleeping with.

Eyes stinging as she stared through the darkness at Alec's face illuminated by the glow of the hurricane lamp, Vanessa realized she'd fallen in love with him. She loved that dark and dangerous streak as much as she loved the honorable man beneath, and she didn't know why she hadn't seen it sooner. She'd been too scared in the shower to connect with the feelings he'd roused from the moment he'd first touched her. But any man who could bring her back from her own private hell the way he had—that man was something special. Something she'd hang onto with both hands.

Wishing Sergio would leave so she could go outside and fling her arms around Alec to tell him how much he meant to her, Vanessa made a visual sweep of the backyard down to the beach. Her gaze drifted over a storage shed in back, the dark shadow of a lawn tractor covered with a tarp and a small stand of trees between Alec's place and the next house over.

A glint in the trees halted her scan, calling her to peer into the area more carefully. The inky blackness of the rest of the yard seemed all the darker in comparison to the ring of light around Alec and Sergio.

Still, Vanessa squinted, body tensing for any possible threat. And as she stared, a shape began to take form. An arm. A leg. And the shiny glint at shoulder level that could only be—

A gun trained on Alec.

ALEC'S INSTINCTS BLARED a warning when Vanessa blasted out of the house, her 9 mm glinting in the moonlight. Only the weapon wasn't trained on Sergio. She pointed into a copse of trees to one side of the property.

"Drop the weapon." Her barked command combined with the mention of a gun had him scrambling out of his seat, reaching for his .357.

If Mark Vercelli or his druggy nephew lurked in those oaks, they were about to be very, very sorry. Quickening his pace, he moved toward Vanessa, only to have Sergio wrench him backward, gripping Alec's gun hand in both of his meaty palms.

Treacherous bastard.

Had it been just the two of them, Alec would have risked the gunshot to take on the older guy. But Vanessa ran right into the range of fire as Sergio grappled for Alec's .357.

"Don't even think about it." Sergio's breath smelled like a mixture of beer and salami. "You know I'll take her out if I have to."

Alec went still, fury raging red-hot through his brain. He watched Vanessa pull Donata Casale out of the trees, still oblivious to Sergio's hold on him.

"Anything happens to her, and I'm not going to care what happens to me. But I guarantee you'll die before I do, old man." Alec forced himself to stay still. He should have trusted Vanessa to do her job. She was a cop, for chrissake. She could handle what came her way.

Instead, his rush to protect her could cost them both their lives. And even though Alec would gladly trade his life for hers, he knew that seeing someone she cared about shot on her watch for the second time would send her back into a dark place she might never be able to recover from.

No way would he do that to her. And damn it, she did care about him, whether she knew it yet or not. He'd been hasty and stupid to push her to acknowledge as much.

Sergio chuckled softly as he kept Alec in front of him in a throat hold and walked them both closer to Donata and Vanessa. "I can't believe you're banging a cop. There's no way in hell we can be related."

Keeping silent, Alec watched Vanessa put a pair of cuffs on Donata before Vanessa glanced back up to Alec. She blinked twice, fast, but other than that, she offered no sign of any reaction. Still, he knew how much that control of hers must cost.

He vowed to find a way out of this for both of them. She wouldn't pay the price for his bad judgment.

"What do you say, Serg?" Vanessa lowered her gun slowly, sizing up Alec's uncle. "You want to trade my prisoner for yours?"

"I think mine is probably a little more dangerous than the cheating whore who's taken to sneaking off with every numb-nut who shows up at the door to work on the house lately."

Donata spit on the ground at his feet. Dark sweats and a long-sleeved T-shirt had replaced the white dressing gown she'd been wearing earlier.

"Those guys are my contacts with the federal government, you moron. I've been working with the feds for months and just tonight I finally got the last piece of information they need to put you away for a long time." She glared over at Vanessa. "I was trying to make sure Sergio didn't shoot Alec, by the way."

"You?" Alec tried to shuffle his vision of Donata as some helpless female trapped in a relationship with a mobster. "What about all that coming on to me you did last fall? I thought you were so scared of Sergio you couldn't stand another day."

She shrugged, her movements clipped and efficient—not at all like the effusive way of gesturing in the role she'd apparently been playing for almost a year. "The FBI is suspicious of you, too. They wanted me to see if I could scrounge up anything to implicate you."

Sergio's grip on the .357 tightened. "You realize you just convinced me to kill you along with these two, don't you?"

Alec hoped his uncle's obvious anger would make him careless. He stared at Vanessa in the moonlight, willing her to work with him when an opportunity arose. The next time they had a chance to act, he'd damn well trust her to do her job while he took care of his.

"Sure thing, Sergio, I just couldn't stand the idea of dying with everyone thinking I was some kind of no-brained mob mistress with nothing going for me."

Alec noticed Vanessa give Donata's arm a reassuring squeeze. An unlikely gesture from an undemonstrative woman whose movements were usually so economical. Efficient.

While Sergio called Donata an assortment of names, Alec half wondered if anyone had some idea in mind for breaking all of them out of this impasse when the soft hum of a car engine moved closer.

Help?

A familiar pair of headlights rolled into the front yard with no regard for the perennial beds. The driver cut the lights, pulling up alongside the stand of trees near the beach.

It was his freaking Mercedes.

Renewed anger fired through him as Mark Vercelli stepped out of the car. *Alec's* car. He couldn't read the license in the dark, but he suspected the guy's new gangster connections had gotten him a fresh set of plates to drive the car around semilegally.

Sergio kept the gun on Vanessa as he held Alec. "Excellent. Our ride is here. Alec, you'll remember my associate Mark since he used to be your associate. The one you assured me would never want to do business with me."

Remaining silent, Alec thought through his and Vanessa's options, knowing they needed to make their break before they went anywhere in the Mercedes. They were as good as dead as soon as they left the house, and he suspected Sergio would just roll the whole car into Long Island Sound, or maybe he'd blow it up with Alec and Vanessa inside. Something to make sure he would never be tied to the "accident."

Alec stared hard at Vanessa, praying their newfound connection, the one that he swore had touched them both deep inside, would somehow help them understand one another now. She slanted her eyes at Donata, then glanced from Sergio to Alec.

Right.

Vanessa would protect Donata. Alec would take out Sergio.

So said his gut instinct. And since he didn't have a choice but to trust it now that Sergio was shoving them all closer to the Mercedes, Alec decided to shut off all the voices inside his head except for one.

The one that told him to go with his gut and trust the woman he loved.

VANESSA HAD SWALLOWED DOWN bile on five different occasions while Sergio held Alec by the throat. But now that she'd looked deep into Alec's eyes, an eerie sense of calm came over her as she walked with numb feet through the sparse grass toward the waiting Mercedes.

Alec trusted her to do her job, to protect Donata and keep herself out of the way of Sergio's firing range. He would make his move any minute, and she would damn well be ready because she would never put him through the hell she'd gone through with Gena. No one was getting shot here tonight, unless it was Mark Vercelli or Sergio Alteri.

She'd already handed Donata—whoever she was— a key to her own handcuffs. Apparently there was no love lost between her and her gangster lover, so Vanessa considered freeing Donata worth the risk.

"You like my new wheels, Messina?" Alec's traitorous partner called as he snapped a wad of gum and waited for Sergio's prisoners to make their way into the back seat.

Vanessa didn't hear Alec's answer, concentrating on picking her moment. They had to move past the patio to get to the car, and as they neared the wrought-iron table, Vanessa heaved herself and Donata to the side.

"I've got a gun strapped to my ankle," Donata called as they hit the cold stone patio blocks together, another gun already sounding in the night.

Tamping down panic, Vanessa patted along the woman's ankles, finding a Smith & Wesson .38 special strapped to her right one. Whatever the hell Donata had been up to tonight, obviously she hadn't been taking any chances.

From the cover of a wrought-iron table they'd toppled onto themselves as they fell, Vanessa watched Alec struggle to regain control of his gun from his uncle. Mark Vercelli stood off to the side, looking unarmed and clueless as he circled the fighting men on the ground.

All the better for her.

Vanessa lined up her shot, ready to protect Alec whatever the cost, but she wasn't going to trip him up by distracting him, either. Alec slammed the gun out of Sergio's hand before landing a knee in his chest.

Mark dove for the gun, but Vanessa's shot beat him to it. She fired into the sand near the .357, scaring Vercelli back about fifty feet.

"I've got him," Donata assured her, slipping out of her cuffs.

With Donata already scrambling to tackle Mark, Vanessa ran toward Alec in time to see him clock his uncle with a patio chair. The wrought iron sent Sergio down for the count and put a sizable dent in the Mercedes.

In the distance, Vanessa could already hear the whirr of police sirens. Donata the federal informant restrained Alec's real-estate partner with the same cuffs she'd been wearing a few moments ago. One day Vanessa would have to ask her about her story—find out how she'd ended up playing a mob boss's girlfriend in exchange for incriminating secrets. But right now, all Vanessa cared about was wrapping herself around Alec.

Flinging her way into his arms, she didn't even mind

when he backed them over to pick up his gun in the sand.

"You kick ass, Vanessa Torres." His words took away any leftover jitters she might have felt, and although she suspected she'd always be scared spitless if someone she loved came under attack, she knew now more than ever that she'd done everything she could to help Gena five years ago. It wasn't about getting even. It was about staying alive.

Still, Alec's words helped. Made her feel like she'd accomplished something important in her time as a detective.

"You kick plenty of your own, Alec." She squeezed his neck tighter, her fingers brushing over the bristly ends of close-cut hair. "And I know now is a really bad time to realize I'm crazy about you, but I am."

She could feel him smile into her hair as he held her.

"I told you so."

"I was just scared to think about it before, but—"

"No buts." He pulled her to his side before two police cars slammed to a halt in his yard. "I was pushing you before and I knew it."

"You're not mad at me?" She dug in the pocket of her jeans for her badge, knowing she needed to go to work before they could finish this conversation in private.

"Hell, Vanessa, I love it that I'm the sensitive one in this relationship." Alec—a dark and dangerous guy with an equally wicked sense of humor—grinned as he kept his gun trained on Sergio.

Damn but she was a lucky woman.

Counting the minutes until she could tell him so, she turned to greet the East Hampton police and help them put away Alec's enemies for a very long time.

THE SUN HAD LONG RISEN by the time the local police cleared them to leave the station. Vanessa rode back to Alec's mini-mansion, spirit lighter than it had been in months as they drove along the waterside route in the Land Rover. The smell of the ocean, the soft warmth of a new spring day wafted through the windows with a sense of promise she hadn't experienced in too many years.

"I can't believe Serg is going to jail for real." Alec's sentiments echoed her own as they pulled into his driveway and parked out in the open. No need to hide in dark garages or subterranean lairs. Alec could now go wherever he wanted without worrying about his uncle's connections breathing down his neck. "He's always weaseled out of everything the cops have ever tried to stick to him."

"No bail. No bucking this one." She slid out of the door, not waiting for Alec to come around. She didn't want him doing too much for the next couple of days since she hadn't convinced him to drop by the hospital and stitch up a knife wound Sergio had managed to inflict during their scuffle.

Men.

"It's the federal case that's going to seal his fate."

Alec disarmed the security system and left it off, holding the front door for her. "Do you believe Donata was helping the feds all this time?"

"She must be fairly well connected for her to have been released so early this morning." Vanessa still wondered how the woman—who swore she wasn't an agent—had managed to get mixed up with Sergio for so long, but after a heartfelt thank you and a goodbye hug, Donata Casale had sailed out of the police station and out of their lives. Vanessa hoped it wouldn't be for good.

"Those disks of financial data are going to help the case, too." Alec reached into the refrigerator for a six-pack of beer that had probably been in there for months. Not that she cared. But then, she'd never made any pretense of being an uptown chick. "So maybe your lieutenant will let you off easy for making up the bomb threat yesterday."

"Are you kidding? He'll be holding that one over my head for years." Lieutenant Russell Durant had put in a call to the local cops to help speed things up for Vanessa. Although he hadn't been happy about her being part of the phony bomb squad and having her plates run by an uptown Manhattan police precinct, at least he'd apologized for landing her hip-deep in trouble with the Alec Messina case. Apparently Russ had known about the federal investigation and hadn't launched a full-scale NYPD effort so as not to step on toes. And since the information was on a "need to know" basis, he hadn't given Vanessa all the details, thinking she'd simply come back to the precinct with an address where they could find their man.

But Vanessa could hardly regret meeting Alec, even if she'd had a few years scared off her life in the process.

"Isn't it a little early for beer?" She checked her watch. "It's 11:00 a.m."

"It's Heineken. I'll have you know that's the champagne of beers." He scooped up a blanket from the back of a rocking chair and held open the back door. "What do you say we toast the new day on the beach before going back to bed?"

"Who knew you were hiding such a romantic side?" Vanessa brushed a kiss over his lips as she passed him. "A toast sounds perfect since I have a few things I've been waiting to say to you, Messina."

"Is that right?" He draped the arm with the blanket over her, cloaking her in the warmth of cotton fleece and sexy man. A very enticing combination. "I might have a few things to say to you, too, now that I think about it."

Little shivers traced up her spine along with his hand. Once they'd crossed a wooden bridge onto the beach, the ocean stretched out in front of them, the endless blue dotted with tiny white boats on the horizon. Seagulls circled and squealed their hungry cries, giving them a wide berth when the newcomers didn't appear to have any food.

"So the fed who showed up at the police station seemed pretty damn impressed with your financial knowledge." Alec spread out the blanket on the sand and then popped open a beer for each of them.

"He just had the hots for me." Vanessa smiled to think how different the charming, talkative agent had been from Alec. "I couldn't tell him all that much until I have a look at the disks for myself."

"But you talk the talk." They settled beside one another on the blanket and Alec clanked his bottle against hers before taking a long first swig. "You could go back into a business field any time you wanted. And I just happen to have a huge, gaping opening in my real-estate company if you're interested."

Vanessa let the magnitude of the offer wash over her as she took a drink of her beer. Not only was Mark Vercelli going to jail, but William McPherson was being questioned in the case as well, since both Mark's and Sergio's testimony gave police reason to think the eldest partner of the firm was involved in the plot against Alec. Chances were excellent Alec would be the sole owner of the company soon.

"That's a huge offer." Vanessa didn't want to offend him, but she'd come to a certain peace with herself and her job through knowing Alec. "And maybe one day when I'm too old to keep up with the bad guys, I'll come begging for that kind of chance. But for now, I think I'm going to stick it out with the police department."

"You're a hell of a cop." He kissed her again, his lips

slightly salty from the ocean breeze and cold beer. "So I guess I can't blame you."

Her heart sped up at his touch, her tired body apparently not too tired to be seriously turned on by this man.

"But I might look into doing some more behind-the-scenes investigative work, too. My sister always says I should put some of the business experience to use to hunt down white-collar crime." And up until now, she'd written off the suggestion every time. "Whatever demon has been chasing me since Gena's accident—I think maybe I put it to rest after the shoot-out today."

"I told you before that I think you'd succeed at whatever you chose to do. I stand by that." He looped his arm around her as they stared out to sea for a long moment, soaking in the warm rays and the warmth of new freedom.

A new connection.

"There was something else I wanted to tell you." Vanessa didn't quite know how to express it now without the adrenaline rush pulsing through her, but the feelings she had inside her from last night were still there. Still one-hundred-percent real. "I don't know what it means, or where we'll take this, but I've fallen for you big time, Alec." Settling her beer bottle into the sand, she curved her hand around his neck and tugged him closer to rest his forehead on hers. "I love you, Messina."

A grin played over his lips, an expression she'd scarcely seen and knew she'd become addicted to soon—right along with that red-hot oil of his he'd used to make her see stars on more than one occasion.

"I'm going down for the count, too, if it makes you feel any better." He flicked his tongue along her lower lip before drawing it between his. "I love you, too."

"You have a house in the Hamptons." A silly concern maybe. Except that Vanessa didn't want to waltz into his life with nothing when he had so much. "I've got a one-bedroom apartment and if I stay in law enforcement, I'll never be able to uphold my half of the Hamptons life-style."

"That's okay. You can spring for the champagne of beers every now and then if you want, but for the most part, I figure it'll be nice to have someone to share my toys with."

Not in a million years would Vanessa have ever con-sidered herself the kind of woman to buy into some Cin-derella fantasy, but she couldn't deny the warm swell in her heart at the thought he would ever be so kind. So generous. So careful to make her feel valued.

"You're a really awesome guy, you know that?"

"Will you still think I'm awesome if I ask you to help me teach my self-defense classes sometimes?" He wrapped a hand around her waist, drawing her closer on the blanket until her leg lined up against his.

"I think I can do that." She'd made her peace with the Bronx after all.

"What if I ask you to go back to the house and have sex with me all day and all night?" His hand dipped under her sweater to skim along her bare back.

"I maintain my stance of being crazy about you."

Heat simmered low in her belly, the fiery emotions giving her surefire proof that Alec had helped her banish all her demons.

His hand skimmed higher. "What if I try to cop a feel of bare breast since you never did put that bra back on after our shower last night?"

"I'd say you're a very dangerous man. And a greedy one at that." She gripped his wrist to hold it steady, her breasts already tightening in response. "But maybe if you're careful not to let anyone see…"

Never a man to let an opportunity pass him by, Alec's hands reminded her exactly how much fun they were going to have together. Fire already leaping inside her, Vanessa arched back to enjoy his touch, thinking she'd be glad to go undercover with him anytime at all.

If you enjoyed what you just read,
then we've got an offer you can't resist!

Take 2 bestselling love stories FREE!

Plus get a FREE surprise gift!

Clip this page and mail it to Harlequin Reader Service®

IN U.S.A.	IN CANADA
3010 Walden Ave.	P.O. Box 609
P.O. Box 1867	Fort Erie, Ontario
Buffalo, N.Y. 14240-1867	L2A 5X3

YES! Please send me 2 free Blaze™ novels and my free surprise gift. After receiving them, if I don't wish to receive anymore, I can return the shipping statement marked cancel. If I don't cancel, I will receive 4 brand-new novels each month, before they're available in stores! In the U.S.A., bill me at the bargain price of $3.99 plus 25¢ shipping and handling per book and applicable sales tax, if any*. In Canada, bill me at the bargain price of $4.47 plus 25¢ shipping and handling per book and applicable taxes**. That's the complete price and a savings of at least 10% off the cover prices—what a great deal! I understand that accepting the 2 free books and gift places me under no obligation ever to buy any books. I can always return a shipment and cancel at any time. Even if I never buy another book from Harlequin, the 2 free books and gift are mine to keep forever.

150 HDN DZ9K
350 HDN DZ9L

Name	(PLEASE PRINT)	
Address	Apt.#	
City	State/Prov.	Zip/Postal Code

Not valid to current Harlequin Blaze™ subscribers.

Want to try two free books from another series?
Call 1-800-873-8635 or visit www.morefreebooks.com.

* Terms and prices subject to change without notice. Sales tax applicable in N.Y.
** Canadian residents will be charged applicable provincial taxes and GST.
All orders subject to approval. Offer limited to one per household.
® and ™ are registered trademarks owned and used by the trademark owner and or its licensee.

BLZ04R   ©2004 Harlequin Enterprises Limited.

Silhouette®

Desire®

presents the next book in

Maureen Child's

miniseries

THREE WAY WAGER

*The Reilly triplets bet they could go
ninety days without sex. Hmm.*

WHATEVER
REILLY WANTS...

(Silhouette Desire #1658)
Available June 2005

All Connor Reilly had to do to win his no-sex-
for-ninety days bet was spend time with the
one woman who wouldn't tempt him. Yet
Emma Jacobsen had other plans, plans that
involved a *very* short skirt and a change
in attitude. Emma's transformation had
Connor forgetting about his wager—but
was what they had strong enough to last
more than ninety days?

Available at your favorite retail outlet.

Arthur was going very deaf and, in exchange for lessons in the fine arts of hunting, fishing and the hurling of abuse, Thermal acted as his rear-gunner whenever they went outside and made sure he was never taken by surprise.

Tigger simply loved him as she loved everyone and everything, and the brand-new kitten swamped him with an adolescent crush that had the entire household squirming in embarrassment. To her Thermal was a cross between Clark Gable and Garfield and he could do no wrong.

And it's easy to see why. He's walking across my desk right this very minute and he's growing into a fine young cat. He has put his childish ways behind him now and that lithe, athletic body has acquired a degree of sophistication and an ease of manner that springs only from self-knowledge and a natural dignity.

But if you'll excuse me, I must be off now – he's got his head stuck in the filing cabinet.